Where Nobody Sees

The track of grass and dry mud took a sharp curve. Immediately ahead of them were the trucks they had heard, tail-lights burning in the darkness, beams illuminating clouds of moths – and something that astounded Luke.

"Steel gates – a fence!" He couldn't believe it. The truck lights turned Furmiston into a stage, and the dominant stage-prop was a twelve foot steel-mesh fence topped with barbed wire.

"It's real. But what the hell's going on through there?" Petra sounded pleased. "Our play's taking shape nicely, but until now – no story."

Luke felt Petra staring at him. "What you're saying is that your story . . ." He pointed through the fence. "Is in there?"

"We'll be needing wire-clippers," she said.

James Watson

Where Nobody Sees

COLLINS

LIONS · TRACKS

The author and publisher gratefully acknowledge permission
to quote from the folllowing:
Lines from 'Heigh-ho, heigh-ho' from Walt Disney's *Snow White*.
Copyright 1937, Bourne Co. U.S.A.
Chappell Music Limited from British Commonwealth and
Empire (excluding Canada and Australasia) and
South Africa. Used by permission.
Lines from *Teddy Bears' Picnic*. Copyright 1907,M. Witmark
& Sons, U.S.A. Sub-published by B. Feldman & Co Ltd. Reproduced
by permission of EMI Music Publishing Ltd, London WC2H 0LD

First published in Great Britain 1987 by Victor Gollancz Ltd
Published in Lions Teen Tracks 1989

Lions Teen Tracks is an imprint of
the Children's Division, part of
the Collins Publishing Group
8 Grafton Street, London W1X 3LA

Printed in Great Britain
by William Collins Sons & Co. Ltd, Glasgow

Chapter 1

The lights blinded Luke. He had come out of a deeper darkness, and into a dream of woods. "Stop it there, son!" He had not run a pace, yet there was no breath in him. He stared into the beams; shielded his eyes.

"Sorry?"

"You looking for something?"

In the middle of oak and birch, approaching an open space before the rough stone track, he had no corner in his dream for traffic, even if it was only one vehicle blocking his way. "Just walking." Stupid way to put it.

"We're wondering just where you're walking, son."

"Home."

"You live in the woods?"

"No – down. . ." A second figure stood behind the headlights; perhaps two more.

"I don't understand."

"We're looking for the fire-raiser, son. Drops his lighted matches on private property."

Don't argue. Beat it. Somebody round here is crazy: fire-raiser? If there had been fires, Luke would have been first to notice.

"Not me."

"Then what brings you on to the moors at quarter to midnight, son?"

Don't like being called 'son', even by Dad. Coming from a stranger, it's an insult.

"What's your name?"

"Are you the police or something?"

"We're something. Now what's your name?" Funny

5

accent. Cockney? A mixture: Aussie, maybe, educated in New Zealand but settled in South Africa. Don't be funny.

"Luke Waller."

"Well, Luke, keep your nose of out these parts after dark. Otherwise –"

"I'm still thinking we should know what he's been up to, Don." The second voice was Belfast Irish; an older deeper voice like the preacher Dad went up the wall about; but deferential to Don.

"I watch badgers," volunteered Luke. "That's all."

Now a duet of laughter. "Badgers – in the pitch dark?"

"Twilight, actually. And then I just sort of sit. And . . ."

"Where are these badgers, son?"

Luke wheeled about. "I'm due home."

"Hey!"

But Luke was running. My name I'll give them, yes. The whereabouts of the badger sett – no. He broke off the track, went over a dry-stone wall and suddenly the only light was that of the moon, momentarily eclipsed by roofs of oak, then shedding a polish of silver on leaves of aspen.

No pursuit. As if it had been a dream, a clip from a gangster movie accidentally stuck into a nature documentary. He headed over Little Moor. The amber lights of Wynster Bridge criss-crossed the valley, then spread in circles up the far hills.

"Bloody cheek!"

"I'm not getting in till I find that earring." Petra was dwarfed by the seven foot copper. "Shine your torch, please, Constable."

"Come on, dumpy – inside!" The policeman had her by the arm.

"Dumpy?" In fury; one precious hoop of real silver lost, and now to be called dumpy. "Don't push – that's assault and very probably battery."

Assault and probably battery it might be, but Petra was tipped into the police van and dropped like laundry between the knees of those already on board. "Budge up, Mother – there's more to come." The van was already full: women in their twenties except for this willowy creature in a blanket; handsome but grey. Petra sat next to her, practically on her.

"Sorry."

"It's okay."

Petra bawled. "It's my citizen's right to search for that earring, Officer Plod."

"Shove the lip, you noisy little bitch, or you'll be charged with a few extras."

This prompted a rich brown voice from the cab-end to say, "Poke your light in somebody else's face, copper. And watch your bloody language – that girl's royalty."

There was a cheer from the others. Taking courage from the support of her comrades. Petra attempted to get out of the van to search for her lost earring. "My sister gave it me." She walked straight on to the policeman's rocketing palm.

"Watch it, stiff-gut!" Black Luce shot from her seat and tipped off the policeman's helmet. Petra was taking a count of five in the gangway of the van.

"Get his number!"

Adrienne, silent till now, gave orders: "Cool it, both of you. Pete – on your bum, please."

PC Plod had caught his helmet. Adrienne's "Sorry, Constable," almost pacified him. "If she's one of yours, just keep a lock on her tongue." To Luce: "And you, you black arsehole, try that again – "

Ruth: "Oh goody, General Rambo's going to nuke us into the next world with his riot shield."

The policeman lunged into the van, across the legs of the woman he had addressed as Mother, but crashed his chin against tall Amy's outsize knees.

"Stack the goods, Dunn," shouted a police sergeant from behind Pete's Plod, Ruth's Rambo, "don't sample them!"

Four vans had swooped. Twenty, maybe thirty police; all stabbing lights and spinning beams. For the Siren Sisters it had been a midnight performance, lit by torches and the bleak floodlights of the perimeter fence, before an appreciative audience of Peace Women. An evening of story and song had been transformed into a melodrama of squealing brakes, crashing doors, shouts, screams, flying bodies, camp fires buried under reversing tyres, benders rammed and clothes lines trampled into dusty mud.

Petra banged ferociously on the police van window. "I've got three brothers who'll come and duff you, copper. And they're all twice as dumpy as me."

The policeman was not happy to let Petra have the last word, though he had no idea what her lips were expressing. He raised two fingers and pressed them against the window.

"Oh hell," said Adrienne, "here we go again."

"You know what this means, son?"

"Please don't call me 'son', Dad."

"Very well, but you know what this means, Luke? – I'll be in plaster for the Carnival."

"It's only a sprain, Dad."

"How do you know if it's not your ankle?"

"You're in pain?"

"Most definitely."

"But you're not in agony."

"Allow me to decide whether falling ten feet from that scaffold has resulted in me suffering agony."

Luke completed the bandaging. "Your socks stink, Dad."

"That makes two of us. They say Michelangelo stank

8

the place out with his socks when he was painting the Sistine Chapel."

They were in Church Hall. Alfred Waller's mural painting on the end wall, entitled WYNSTER BRIDGE – PAST, PRESENT AND FUTURE, was almost finished.

"What happened?"

"I reached out to scrub some obscene graffiti composed by persons unknown – and wallop! What do you think?"

Luke stared up at the painting, teeming with people and events. "It's getting out of date. At least three of my friends you've got in there have left."

"Then a bit of them will stay here for ever. Come on, help me up." Alfred stood on one leg, leaning heavily on Luke. "I'm a useless old derelict."

Luke nodded. "You take on too much. I read in a book, it's a form of hysteria. You go round in circles, faster and faster. Burn yourself out."

"What else is there to do?" Together they hobbled out of Church Hall, up the rear steps and into the hot night air. Sahara Summer they were calling it – not a drop of rain for weeks; blue skies as eternal as holiday brochures; suntans so common people had given up wanting them.

"Tea, Dad?" asked Luke as they entered the stone-floored kitchen of Church House.

Alfred was pensive. He stared uneasily at his son. "Listen, I know what you're thinking."

"No you don't, Dad."

"At least have the good grace to let me guess: about you, me – your mother . . . I've been meaning, well, to talk."

"Talk?" Luke had filled the electric kettle. He switched on.

"About everything. Get things off our chests. Somehow I just find . . . it difficult to get started. You see, son – "

Luke winced, but went on making the tea. You see, son

9

– that's how it always started. Dad forgets; thinks we've never talked. Yet we've gone over it all till the cows come home. Round and round in ever decreasing circles: don't blame Vera; don't be bitter or resentful.

"You see, grown-ups . . ."

"Dad, I'm absolutely pooped. Can we leave it till morning?"

"What about the paper-round?"

"Later, then."

"When you're back from work? There's never a good time, Luke . . . I just don't want you blaming her."

"Blaming *her*?"

"Or blaming me for that matter."

Luke thrust a mug of tea in front of Alfred. He put in two spoonfuls of sugar and did the stirring. "You'll need a hand getting upstairs."

"You won't discuss it?"

"Come on, Michelangelo – up those stairs."

"You treat me like a child."

"Yes, Dad . . ."

"My name's Pete, what's yours?" Petra Scales had warmed to the quiet grey-haired woman; so lost, yet who had been determined to be arrested along with the others.

"Vera."

"How long?" The bright light of the police cell revealed Adrienne's theatrical make-up, half a white face, half a black one.

"At the fence? Oh, four months, a little more."

"Where're you from?" Ruth's make-up was half red, half yellow.

"Up north. I was enjoying your show. It was so nice to laugh. I'd almost forgotten . . ."

The others nodded, pleased.

"And you, do you get arrested much?"

Adrienne held up crossed fingers. "Only when we run out of luck. It's bad for business. You can't run a theatre group from behind bars."

Vera asked if all the Siren Sisters had been arrested. "All that count," said Luce. "But we've our houseboy Ron out there somewhere."

"Riding to our rescue!" laughed Petra.

Amy, six feet, timid as a mouse except when a musical instrument was in her hands, asked, "Will they keep us inside?"

Petra had dropped her head on Adrienne's shoulder. A hand rose to gather in copper curls. "Not the kids, maybe."

"I'm eighteen going on nineteen," murmured Petra, the only one of the Siren Sisters not to be plastered with make-up.

"You're seventeen going on seventeen," reminded Adrienne. "And there's a chance they might classify you as a mitigating circumstance and grant you your liberty."

"Then I'll refuse – because I don't want to be separated from you lot."

"Allow us to decide that, Junior," smiled Ruth.

In the small hours. Vera alone remained awake. She envied the closeness of her prison friends. "They're all of a piece," she thought. She dozed, and her first dream was of home. Strange, for in the dream was Petra, perched on a dry-stone wall. She was making her son laugh.

"Who'll you be sleeping with tonight, dreamboat?"

Luke removed his gaze from the skylight in the factory roof to the work he was doing – lifting tins of white gloss as they raced along the track, twisting them with an aching wrist and with the other hand stamping them with the trademark of Monarch Paints, a stag with outspread antlers. Automation had been slow to catch on in Wynster Bridge.

He opened his mouth, then shut it.

"With his blue eyes he ought to have no bother with the girls," said Freda, mother of five and lately a grandmother, scooping up tins and stacking them on a wooden pallet beside her.

"He's keeping his counsel by the looks of things." Ellen, the original questioner, was in charge of the paint-flow at the machine end. She was Monarch's Miss Hollywood, mother of twins whom Alfred had portrayed as angels in his Church Hall mural.

Luke had been thinking about last night: who were those people? What right had they to bar his way, interrogate him, shine torches in his face? Who did they think they were? And on my patch.

"Not telling, are you?" Ellen persisted. She gave Luke a wink. "Or are ministers' sons not supposed to do it?"

All the girls laughed. Loudest was Madge, five years running unisex darts champion at the Rising Sun. Her job in the rota was to check that the lids were properly fixed by giving each tin a hearty smack with a mallet. "Sundays is for praying, Luke," she grinned. "And Fridays is for something else." She gave him a nudge with her hip. "And not sideways, either!"

"You made him smile, Madge," observed Freda, crashing tins on tins.

"He's admitting nowt."

"But he's blushing like a roast turkey."

"You know what?" Madge announced. "I think our Luke's a v-i-r-g-i-n . . . You know what one of them is, Luke?"

Luke stared at his friendly tormentors. He was well used to teasing because people often decided he was a bit slow; always hesitant in answering questions as though he had to work out which order to put the words in.

Once he had realised how slow off the mark he

could be, he became self-conscious, which made him worse. Gradually he had learnt to cope and these days was only caught out by unexpected questions. A tactic he had adopted to give himself time to think was to repeat the question slowly. "A virgin, Madge?"

"Yes, a virgin, Luke. You been told about virginity, have you?"

He took a four-second pause and was ready. Straight-faced, eyes modestly averted, he answered, "My History teacher, Miss Creasey, explained it to me."

"Oh?" Their ears were in their eyes. Luke kept stamping the tins.

"Surely," began Ellen, suspecting she was exchanging an ace for a joker, "you mean your Biology teacher?"

"Definitely Miss Creasey."

"And what did she say?"

"She didn't *say* anything, as I recall."

Even the paint-filled machine seemed to mute its hiss, plop and clunk to listen. "All I know is they wouldn't let me into the sixth form."

Madge's eyes bulged with disbelief. "What are you on about? That Miss Creasey is forty-five if she's a day."

Luke continued his stamping, sensing the laughter welling up in the women who stared at his thin but neat-packed frame as though he had stepped out of his clothes. "I was too polite in those days," he sighed, "to ask how old she was."

Madge threw back her head. "Don't you go tellin' them daft tales to your mam, Luke Waller!"

Foreman Bill Gordon interrupted the party. He shouted from the office, "Phone for you, Luke."

Madge whooped. "It's that Miss Creasey – she's just had triplets!"

It was Dad in a panic. "You'd better come home right away, son."

13

"They'll dock my wage, Dad."

"It's your mother. She's gone and got herself arrested."

"Silence in court!" It was a long while coming, for the courtroom was packed. Luke sat squashed in the public gallery. He clutched his wallet pocket which contained the last of the Waller household savings – exactly £50. The whole Peace Camp appeared to have turned out to support the forty accused.

There was no sign of Vera.

The benches below the public gallery had been cleared of solicitors and the press to make room for so many late additions to the charge-sheet. Prisoners were still being filtered in, mostly women, cheerful and defiant. The occasional males of the species looked sorry and bewildered as if they'd been caught loitering in the magistrates' lavatory.

Luke had argued with his father about who should come to pay Vera's fine. This was after an argument whether either of them had any right to pay her fine in the first place. "Dad, she *wants* to get locked up for her beliefs. That's the point. That's her right."

"What about our rights?"

"Not sure what you mean."

"To love and protect her?"

"But what if she doesn't want love and protection?"

Alfred was stung. "I shall go and pay. It's what I want to do and feel is right, whatever she says."

"Not on that ankle – how could you?"

"Then I'm at your mercy."

Luke decided there was no harm in offering to pay Vera's fine so long as it was an offer not a bribe. "I'll take the money. I'll be there."

His father had relaxed a fraction. "Tell her ... tell her she's missed. And we want her back."

"She comes back, Dad – one week in every ten. That was her promise."

"You know what I mean – back for good."

I'll do no such thing. Luke scanned the faces. A bigger crowd than Wynster Athletic gets in a whole season. More like a theatre than a courtroom, for in the front row of the accused stood five women in a variety of costumes.

Their faces were made up in contrasting colours. One wore an Afro-style orange wig; another a head-dress of ostrich feathers; another, tall as a flagpole, was smothered in bands of jewellery and beads as though she had played King Solomon or the Queen of Sheba. Or, as Luke surmised, there being so few in the company, Solomon and Sheba together.

Yet it was the girl in the middle, without make-up, but with a wealth of copper hair, who hooked Luke's interest. She was younger than her companions, fair-skinned, quick-smiling.

Green eyes, got to be. And probably freckles. Spring leaves, autumn leaves.

Unlike the rest of the group, the girl was dressed for everyday; obviously a biker, with a zip leather jacket, much worn, covered in badges, with tassels from the wrists to the elbow. Round her throat was a blue-tinted white scarf which at Monarch Paints they would have named Eskimo Dawn. There were bangles on each wrist in a rainbow of colours, and she wore one very large earring, as big as those they put through bulls' noses.

The magistrates had taken their seats. There was a simmering buzz of voices, gradually fading, when all at once a member of the public elbowed her way to her feet and yelled at the court:

"Shame on British justice . . . You arrest the peacemakers and let the warmongers go free!" She sat down abruptly. There was a burst of applause and a chorus of support.

15

The court rang with slogans. At least ten speeches were started. Somebody began to sing the opening of *We Shall Overcome*. Feet stamped.

"Silence in court!" cried the court usher, sporting a horrible vein in his temple. Suddenly the court was filled with policemen.

Luke's backbone shrank. His head ducked, like at school when Old Dracula was on the blood-hunt for victims, fangs dripping: "You boy!" That was your Polaris, Cruise and Trident rolled into one. "You boy – see me after Assembly!" The blood of innocent and guilty alike would freeze. So here in court Luke stayed with neck concertinaed into body, eyes looking along his nose as four policemen waded in among the public gallery crowd to remove the hecklers.

After deafening noise, deafening silence. Nobody volunteered for execution. The police retreated, issuing dire warnings.

And yet, as soon as proceedings got under way again, a woman beside Luke, who had not spoken or moved and seemed to be actually asleep inside the hood of her camping jacket, took action. She slipped a huge football rattle from a Sainsbury's bag and whirled it round in the air.

Just as swiftly, she dropped the rattle between her legs only for it to land square at Luke's feet. The eyes of a policeman at the end of the row struck Luke's gaze with the penetration of a *Star Wars* laser. He came for Luke.

"Not me ... It wasn't ..!" He was grasped by the hair and nose-dived forward.

"Pick it up!" He did. The fist was in his neck, then the iron claw closed up his collar. He was punched in the side just under the ribs. People thought they were helping by holding Luke, so that for a moment he feared he would be snapped in two. "Not me!"

He was over knees. His private parts collided with the armrest at the end of the bench. His feet were nowhere near the ground. He was carried, head first, against the handle of the swing door. Outside, he was stood up. A knee in the groin exploded not only where it hurts most, but in all of him – head, gut, spine, the back of his legs, and he crashed against brown tiles, slipping.

On the point of going down the stairs back first, Luke grabbed the rail, thought the police were coming for him again and flinched. He turned, stumbled and fell over his own feet.

"It wasn't me!" No one heard his protestation, for he was alone on the stairs. In agony – yes Dad, this is agony – he sat on a step. He clutched himself round his knees. Not bleeding and no teeth missing. Be thankful for small mercies. He shoved out one leg, then the other. The pain eased a fraction.

It had been, as they say, a friendly warning. He gasped. He levered himself up. He felt for his wallet: still there. He shivered. He leaned on the stair rail. He rubbed himself gently. He began a tortured descent to the exit. He was thinking about what Madge had said yesterday. This can't have done much for my virginity.

In expectation of the ending of proceedings, people had begun to gather on the court steps and in the car park. They were mainly young men and women with something to say – holding placards and banners; and something to sell – newspapers, booklets, leaflets, badges and tee shirts urging the public to PROTEST AND SURVIVE.

"Waller? The minister's wife?" The counter clerk glanced down the chargesheet. "She's not been charged."

Luke stepped out into the stifling midday sun. She was free, but she had spent the night in custody. That'll please Dad. And we've saved money. He knew she would be in court somewhere; probably pleading to be booked like the others.

He sat on the court steps wondering whether you could be put in prison these days for not paying the electric. Dad hadn't paid, and he'd received a Final Warning. The gas had been paid for with the proceeds from Luke's two-stroke motorcycle. Dad's M-reg Dyane went to cover the rates, while the twintub helped take the sting out of the Water Board.

Yes, Vera's teacher's pay, modest though it was, had been dearly missed.

School was loose: out came the hordes, squeezing through the pinned-back doors in a blaze of noise. They were greeted with cheers and waving placards. Pigeons dodged the foot-traffic, then took fright and soared over to silent gardens.

Luke felt his arm grasped. "I'm terribly sorry." His lady neighbour in the public gallery was going at his elbow as if it were an old water pump. "I never intended you should carry the can for my rattle . . . if you see what I mean."

He was surrounded. "It's okay . . . okay."

"They roughed you up, didn't they?"

He was moving, pushing. "Mum!"

Vera was thrusting down the court steps, steaming and waving. "Luke."

Free of Miss Rattle, Luke met his mother in the hot press of the crowd; good, the feeling, arms about one another. Not angry like last time; even pleased to see him. Wonderful to see her.

"They refused to charge me. I'm disgusted." He pulled back in pain as she clasped his head. "What's up?"

"Got a knock."

She examined him. "That's nasty. Been fighting?" She smiled at her own joke. "Course not – my boy's a pacifist, right?"

18

It was always the same: awkward questions, impossible answers. "I'm not – "

"Listen – did you bring cash?"

"Cash?"

"You're at it again, Luke Waller. How many times have I to tell you? Repeating people's questions is a fault you ought to be growing out of."

"Yes, Mum."

"*Vera*. I've told you: I've a name. People I like call me Vera." She was going for his wallet pocket. "Quick then."

He brushed her hands away. "I'll do it."

"Then do it!"

"How did you know I'd got cash?"

"Because it's the kind of trick your father gets up to. How much?"

Remembering the unpaid electricity bill, he lied: "Thirty quid."

"Thirty pieces of silver, more like."

He counted out thirty pounds in fivers.

"Great. This'll pay Petra's fine. Now you wait here. Believe it or not, your father's at last done something useful." She turned and ploughed through the crowd.

Why do I always let her bully me?

Vera was away twenty minutes. The crowd had almost dispersed when she swept once more on to the stage in a flurry of triumph, pushing ahead of her the girl with the copper hair. Arm slung in arm, they came down the steps. "Petra – or Pete, rather – this is Luke, my sole venture into childbirth. For whom Vera Waller is a great disappointment."

"The badger-gazer?"

Away they went, the red taps of embarrassment. He stuck out his hand woodenly and felt it shaken with vigour. "Heard all about you," Petra said, "at three o'clock this morning."

Vera: "Locked in a police cell, Luke, with your disgrace of a mother. What'll they be saying about that in Wynster, do you think? A minister's wife!"

Luke shrugged. Not very much, probably. They're used to her.

"Well, you tell them – I loved every minute of it." Vera gave Petra a hug which almost pulled her off her feet. "The other four in the party said Can't Pay, Won't Pay, so they're in for ten days, which leaves Pete at a loose end. Not to worry, it's all arranged."

"All arranged?"

"There you go again, Luke," Vera was too pleased with herself to scold him further. "Pete's a member of the – what do you call yourselves, Pete?"

Petra's smile was even more luminous than it had been in court. The copper of her hair was reflected in her face – a mass of freckles attempting a suntan over her nose and forehead. There was a slight gap between her two front teeth. Dissecting her right eyebrow, an old scar broke the gingery symmetry of her features. Her eyes were, as Luke had guessed them to be, a deep green; like rhododendron leaves and, Luke thought, as spiky.

"The Siren Sisters."

"They do plays to promote greater understanding of other countries," Vera explained.

"And a lot more."

"Listen, Luke . . ." Come to think of it, mused Luke, this was one of Vera's bad habits she ought to be growing out of. Whenever she was going to be provocative or dictatorial, she began her statement with "Listen . . ." And Luke had got into the bad habit of answering, "I'm listening," which somehow irritated Vera as much as him repeating her questions.

"Listen," she said. Luke held back from his usual comment. Instead he looked at Pete. Some Pete! "Your

20

father will be thanking me on bended knees ... I've signed up the Sirens for his Grand Carnival. Now how about that?"

Luke stumbled once more into bad ways. "Booked them?"

"Yes, to bring some light and life to Wynster Bridge. Shake the place up a bit. Bulldoze their brains."

"But ... Dad can't – "

"Afford them? Tell the child, Pete."

"It's a street theatre, you see. We live on collections. And we sell things."

"Pete's coming back with you to get everything organised. She can have the spare room. See that you air the sheets and blankets properly."

"But – "

"One more 'but', buster, and I'll have your butt over my knee, big as you are. Now listen." Vera listed the benefits a live threatre group would bring to what she termed a 'dead-head' town such as Wynster. "What's more, Pete here will be a tonic for the Waller household – and don't say 'What's left of it!' The fact is, you and your dad have become stale."

"Stale?"

"Yes, like a couple of octogenarians in a geriatric ward."

As the World Champion Arranger (Luke's judgment), Vera arranged a lift back to the Peace Camp. She arranged a feast of broth and unsugared tea for her son, Petra and a dozen friends she had made during her four months under canvas and stars.

Luke sat, numb as an octogenarian in a geriatric ward; only this was Vera's bender, a makeshift tent strung between two poles. He had been up at four, finished his paper-round at six, caught a six-thirty train, then an eight o'clock bus. He had been dragged from the court, used as a battering ram through the swing doors and suffered a knee in the crutch. In short, he was feeling eight years old and completely geriatric – whatever that meant. Must look it up.

Only later was he to recall fragments of his visit to Vera's new home: smoke plumes from the camp fires, songs, people snug in battered armchairs and three-legged sofas; signs everywhere, strung along the fence, between the branches of trees – great spiders' webs of bright-coloured cloth, string, Christmas wrapping tape, streamers, and everywhere photographs of loved ones, mostly children: other sons and daughters left behind for the cause.

He was to recollect the deep tyre tracks, now caverns of parched mud, battleground of countless struggles between the protestors and the protectors of the fence. He remembered the concrete posts, angled at the top, strung with the latest razor wire. Like pictures of concentration camps. He sensed, too, the eternal waiting. "A war of patience," somebody said. "The Government thinks that if it waits long enough, we'll get tired and go home."

"Like hell," had been the chorus.

Luke was sent off for water at a stop-tap. He looked across at the police on duty inside the weapons base. They were clad in Wellington boots despite the heat, and their Alsatians sat with their tongues hanging out, desperate for shade. Luke wondered, who are the prisoners?

"Very peaceful, isn't it?" Petra had strolled up behind him.

"Peaceful?" There I go again.

"Not over there ... but the Peace Village." She sounded as awkward as he did.

Luke was surprised at himself. Normally, faced with a beautiful girl, he seized up like his old two-stroke used to do. He became a goldfish, all flapping mouth but no words. On this occasion he felt at ease. Perhaps it was the badge on her biker's jacket which said, IF YOU DON'T BITE ME, I'LL NOT BITE YOU. "Is it – peaceful, I mean?"

"Not really. Not at night, anyway. Everything's okay, then all at once you get the yobs in the dark."

"Yobs – the police?"

Petra shook her head. "Patriots . . . You know, the type who are nuts in the head. Bullies, usually cabbage-brains, full of pub courage and Union Jack tattoos. They trample the tents, beat up the girls."

Luke felt it might be the right moment to offer an apology. "I'm sorry if Vera's . . . I mean, if she's well – "

"Done a hijack on us?"

"She's no right to go inviting you up . . . to Wynster Bridge of all places." He grinned. "The only street theatre we've ever had was a gas explosion in Peabody Street. What's worse, everybody's stony-broke."

Petra glanced down at her jacket. She returned Luke's smile. "There's always an answer in my badges – here you are." She thrust her thumb under a badge. It read GO FOR BROKE.

"You believe that?"

"All the way . . . Anyhow, we *are* broke. The Sisters couldn't pay their fines even if they wanted to."

"Didn't the Siren Sisters lure passing sailors to their doom?"

She laughed. "That's just the interpretation men put on the story. We prefer to think the Siren voices spoke of peace and love. Neither are good for business as that guy Odysseus found out . . . Course, our houseboy Ron prefers to call us the Foghorns." She sighed. "They stopped our Arts Council grant ages ago, and we've no bookings for a month – so why not get another explosion going in Peabody Street?"

"You'll find us the most stagnant backwater this side

23

of the Dead Sea. Nothing's ever happened since Oliver Cromwell."

"That's something."

"Not really. He took one look at the place and stepped back. To commemorate the event, they named the valley Stepback."

Petra was not discouraged. She shoved out another badge. It said, WE HAVE WAYS OF MAKING THINGS HAPPEN. "See what I mean?"

"Cloth ears!" Luke hadn't caught Vera's words. She repeated them with mock exasperation. "You won't be needing your return ticket, so cash it as soon as you get home."

"Won't need it?"

"Luke, I've just said, haven't I – Pete will be providing the transport. Got that?"

He nodded, overcome by depression. Two hundred miles on a pillion seat behind a woman driver: the experience could scar him for life. "I've no helmet," he declared, sensing a line of escape.

"That's arranged. There's a spare back at the barge."

"Barge?"

"Our place." Petra decided it was time to chivvy Luke up. "It's worth a visit if you don't mind a bit of mud in your eye . . . And I need to pack and arrange things with Ron. Okay?"

He had no alternative. "Okay." I'm trapped. Vera's about to spill my intestines if I say another word.

"Pete might even let you drive on the quiet roads."

Great.

Vera interrupted her farewell hug with a warning. "Now remember, Pete's in your safe-keeping. Tell Alfred I'll be up for his wonderful carnival." She paused. "Other commitments permitting."

He was impressed, even stood back to take in the

polished lines of the 350 cc Norton Navigator. Petra watched him. "Like Nortons?"

For an antique, it was in perfect condition. "You don't like them, you worship them . . . do you?"

"Service it, repair it, re-fit it, spit-and-polish it – yes!" She laughed, pleased. "Join the club."

"But – "

"Used to be my dad's. Climb on board." After a short burst on a metalled road, Petra swung off and began to cross open country. Her "Hold tight!" was the most unnecessary statement of the year. They were on cart-tracks centred with thick grass; paved, where the tractors passed, with broken stone and half-bricks.

He admitted it, she was good. To even keep a grip of the handlebars at this speed, over this terrain, was an achievement. At first he had considered steadying himself with the steel frame of the pillion. After two hairpin bends he decided to clutch on to her. Not bad at all. Right round her tight leather waist. A real bonus. He tucked his head into her shoulder: one eye shut in fear, the other open in amazement (and fear).

"What?" She had called something into the whip of the evening wind. He guessed it must have been 'Short cut'. Across a cornfield which had just been harvested, between towers of hay bales steeped in blue shadows, through a gate and back on to splattering half-bricks, then bang up a slope which suddenly stopped being a slope and became a descent between hedges.

"What?" He guessed this time: ahead, the blue-grey rim of a canal. The machine bounced. Luke bounced, and the sharpness of the bounce reminded him he was still in pain from this morning.

"What?" Now it was her turn to guess at his cry of "Steady!" No point in trying to explain. Petra opened the throttle towards the homeward rise.

To the left of them, about half a mile along the towpath, was the stubby hulk of a canal barge. The track zig-zagged up to the bank. Luke yelled – no, yelped – for it looked as if Petra aimed to span the canal with one gigantic acceleration. He closed both eyes. Thank God I can swim.

The Norton took both slope and bend with wheels alternatively on and off the ground; but the water was beside them, not all over them. "Okay?" This Luke understood: Okay? Am I okay? He decided an answer was not required. It was what Stanley Reeves, his old English teacher, used to call a 'rhetorical question'.

Petra dropped her head towards the bars, leaving Luke full face in the blast of wind. So he dropped with her. At the same instant she raised her back, almost sweeping him off the pillion and into the canal.

And then she stopped, causing only a modest dust storm around the Navigator's rear wheel. She doffed her helmet, shook out her hair and said, "There."

Luke put both feet on solid earth. He felt recognisably alive. He paid particular attention to keeping his balance, and looking casual. He didn't speak in case there was a rattle in his voice.

Petra laid her helmet carefully on the seat of the Navigator. "Now I'd like you to wait here, Luke. Ron's a bit touchy, being the only man around. Ruthy calls him Firework because he's worse than a ten quid rocket when ignited." She smiled, genuinely nervous at the prospect of this encounter with the Siren Sisters' universal handyman. "He requires coaxing." She shrugged. "Which is Adrienne's job usually, not mine."

"What?" This was the fourth 'What?' of the journey, but by far the loudest. It came from inside the barge, specifically from the forward end, which Luke had examined with a stir of interest.

Named *The Lucky Dragon*, the canal barge was thickly

26

surfaced with pitch. The upper portions were striped in yellow and black and separated from the black lower half with a scarlet band running from stem to stern. On top of the cabin area was a multi-coloured sign, THE SIREN SISTERS. Above this a rope was strung from a mast at one end to another midships, bearing flags of nations of the world.

"What?" roared Ron Kemp, unseen, to 'coaxing' words from an unseen Petra, which were plainly not coaxing enough. "All of them?" His voice burgeoned out upon the tranquil landscape of whispering willows and a blackbird celebrating the end of a perfect day. "And nobody bothered to let me know? You're pillocks, the lot of you – what are you? Listen!"

Obviously Petra was listening for no sound came from her quarter. Ron went on. "I wipe your noses and your arses for you. I make life on board this Ship of Fools tolerable and possible – and what do you do to me? As soon as my back's turned, you land the whole kaboozle into porridge. We're finished, that's what we are. Trashed up. We might as well jack everything in and shove off to the nearest dosshouse."

Ron's temper kept on rocketing into the biosphere. "And didn't I warn you? If just once more you tangled with the Law – didn't I promise, so help me? Just once more, and it was goddamn cheerio from me."

There was a silence lasting a full minute, then:

"You've WHAT?"

This fifth 'What?' provoked the blackbird to take its gladsome song to a more appreciative audience across the canal, among loosestrife and snapdragons.

"Booked us in where . . .?" Ron had begun jumping up and down; either that, or he was striking something hard with something harder. "Never heard of the place

27

. . . Shush? What the hell do you mean, shush?" Another gap in the harangue. "Where?"

Luke braced himself. It was his turn. He gazed towards the open cabin door above which, in a wire basket, was a flourish of pink geraniums. Judging by the volume of Ron's voice, Luke expected somebody like his pal Ivan, who'd gone to London to be a nightclub bouncer. Instead, out stepped a dapper elf of a man, brown hair twisted into a single plait which reached almost to his waist. He wore rimless glasses, a white, sleeveless cotton shirt with SAVE THE WHALE printed on the front and tight red cords chopped off below the knee. There was a chunky brass bracelet on one wrist and a chain made of coins on the other. His bare arms were tattooed, though Luke was too far away to see their detail.

Ron stared at Luke with interest, but he was still angry. He turned to Petra. "What's he – a peace offering?"

A prickly and resolute reply came from Petra. "Luke's in my safe-keeping. Ron. And he's being very patient with everybody." She paused. Her next comment was nicely calculated to deflect Ron from his irritation. "And you might be of a mind to learn that Luke's an authority on badgers."

"Badgers!" Ron's mood changed instantly. He scratched his chest. He came forward, wiped his hand and held it out in greeting to Luke. "You've seen them in the flesh – the real thing?"

Luke stood at ease, smiled. "There's a family I watch, most evenings. Parents and a couple of cubs. They're magic." Ron welcomed him aboard, putting an arm round his shoulder.

Inside the barge there was a clash of smells: tar versus curry; linseed oil versus the yeasty odour of home-brewed beer. The step down into the forward section of the barge opened into the neatest, minutest threatre imaginable. "Enough for twenty souls, Luke . . . See." Ron picked up a wooden plank stacked with others along the ship's side. "Designed all this myself." He laid the plank crosswise in craftsman-cut slots. "Plonk your bum on that. Thirty pence extra for a cushion."

Ron was still sharp with Petra: "Don't think you're getting away with this, kiddo."

"Something to eat, Luke?" she asked, unperturbed.

Ron: "Yes, you buzz off and put the kettle on."

Petra went up a step through the stage area. Ron followed, clutching Luke's elbow. "Voilà! Lights, foot and flood. Roller screen for my lantern slides – best collection on water."

"It'd be a bit difficult doing *Romeo and Juliet* in here," ventured Luke, standing in a blaze of lemon spotlight.

"Most of our performances are outdoors . . . *their* performances, I should say, the Sirens. I just make things possible. The crude mechanic . . . And here, back-stage, the sleeping quarters. Fitted the bunk beds myself. Amy sewed the curtains."

He pointed ahead at a plastic shower curtain. "That's the galley where I do most of the cooking. The Foghorns, as I prefer to call them, are useless at the culinary arts. Adrienne can do a decent omelette, but the rest are frozen food merchants. Their first and last cooking utensil is a tin opener."

Ron beckoned Luke to sit down at the narrow dining table. "Real oak . . . Mind you, to do her justice, it's Amy who works out the stage lighting for me. She's a diploma or something in Electronics . . . She's my favourite because she listens instead of yapping all the time." He lowered his voice, nodding towards the galley where Petra was pouring out tea. "That one's the worst yapper of the lot. Between you and me, Luke, I'd have her off the ship."

He shrugged. "But they all love her, so what's the use

of making bad blood?" He relented, smiling very faintly. "I guess I love her a bit myself, but that doesn't make her any less of a ruddy nuisance – ah, char up!"

To accompany the pint mugs of tea, Petra served doorstep slices of malt loaf, plastered with butter. "You can tell a miner's daughter when you see one, Luke." He raised his chunk of malt loaf. "You'd not miss this in the dark!"

For a so-called yapper, Petra proved untrue to form. She sat down. She said nothing, leaving the stage for Ron. "And you're in this lass's safe-keeping, eh, Luke? Then God help you." He reached up to a head-high locker, fitted by himself, and took out a map. He flicked a hand through Petra's copper hair. "Still, you'll not die of boredom, that's for sure."

Ron spread out the map. "Now, tell us exactly where your Badgerville is."

Chapter 2

"Okay?"

"Yes, okay." Homeward bound, so it was okay. And good to be on the machine again. At sixty-five, summer wind stopping up the eyes. Lights burning southwards, whipping through half-closed lids, stirring memories of life on the two-stroke: deep breaths down caverns of space; over Snape Ridge above Furmiston Forest, taking off, floating around the pebble shore of Boldventure Lake, rousing gulls and waders from fish dinners; singing over his shoulder like on that last climbing trip to the Roaches.

All seems a century ago.

They had taken one tea-stop at a motorway café. While chewing pizza, Luke's chauffeur poured out tea and her life story. Well, half of it. We've another stop before the turn off when I'll get the other half.

Petra: "Can't last an hour without strong tea. No sugar, spoils a noble beverage. I could say *au revoir* to beer any day – but tea, that's special. Spiritual even. My dad was a Kentish miner. He drank gallons of the stuff. When he died we sold his inside to the India Tea Centre. His lungs we got nothing for, of course; there's no market for coal dust.

"I miss him. Sometimes when I can't call up his voice, I think of his cough. Got on all our nerves when he was alive. It'd be a symphony to me now.

"Snowdown, a lovely name for a pit. Getting to the coalface was like travelling on the trans-Siberia express blindfolded. It stretched so far, Dad promised it would eventually come up right under the Houses of Parliament. Then we'd have the revolution!

31

"Forty-six years man and boy, digging his way to Westminster and – do you know – I earned as much in my second job, selling silver fox furs to the clueless upper-crust in Bond Street.

"There were six of us, three of each. My brothers are big as oil rigs – all swanned off to foreign parts, and doing well. My sister Gabrielle's in the States, and Lena in London, married to Sam who works in industrial films. They've just had a little boy, given him my dad's name, Michael.

"I was little Miss Afterthought. Ten years behind the rest, which ruined me horribly. Can you imagine Christmas with that lot, then my brothers' wives? Course in the last years there was only Mum, Dad and me. They died within four months of each other. On my sixteenth, my dad took me to motocross over at Arlington. On the return trip, he handed me the keys. 'You get us home safe, pet,' he said, 'and the machine's yours.' The happiest day of my life."

Luke had been impressed by the condition of the Norton and tried to keep his pupils from dilating in surprise as Petra described how she stripped the machine down; listed the parts she had replaced or restored. She did her dad proud.

"At school I was useless because I could never see the point and kept asking 'Why do we have to do this, sir?' A pain in the rump, I guess. Their snapping out together knocked me sideways.

"I had nine jobs in eight months. Got engaged once, to a weight-lifter with the most perfect body in the world . . . That lasted a fortnight till I discovered he voted Tory and went to Mass on Sunday. I squatted, dossed under Charing Cross Bridge for a week, and then joined the mobile soup kitchen as salter, stirrer and server . . .

"From whence I graduated, after scrubbing my nails, to the fresh-cream truffle counter of one of the capital's snobbiest stores, resort of duchesses, vice-regents and TV

32

celebrities. Couldn't make my mind up which was the most insufferable. They treated us like shit.

"Took my revenge, though. The only person who got what he paid for was a tramp who insisted on having two truffles tied up in a box. So I weighed in with two pounds of the things, plus a free ribbon. Those who smiled or said 'Please' got fifty per cent more than they asked for. The others got fifty per cent less.

"You know, they came dripping with diamonds and half the animals in the world's remaining forests draped over their backs. They could afford everything twice over. Except 'Please' and 'Thank You'.

"What decided me to chuck in the towel happened the day there were more headlines of world famine. On the Saturday we sold fifteen thousand quid's worth of chocolates. That night I went out with the idea of getting tanked up to the ears. Instead, I ended up at the open-air show of the Siren Sisters.

"I tell myself Dad spoke to me. Course I don't believe in the after-life. But whispers, yes. As if people you love go on living in your head. If you let them.

"Siren Sisters! They were like a door from Hell to Heaven. I waited till the audience had all gone. I went up to Adrienne – and I chucked myself on the ground, as if I'd got St Vitus' Dance combined with the Curse of Montezuma. I begged them not to move me till I'd recovered. No doctor, I said. No ambulance. Just a lie-down and a cuppa tea.

"The Sisters were all round me. Ruthy, Luce, Amy, Ron in a cussed temper as usual; and not a single cream truffle between them. They lifted me on to *The Lucky Dragon*. It was summer, but not a sauna summer like this one.

"Adrienne gave up her bunk for me and suddenly I felt a fake, the world's number one con-woman. I was about to apologise and confess when, right out of the blue

– or grey, actually, because it had started to rain – we got raided by this mob from the British Party, or whatever it's called, all bulldogs and bovver boots.

"Paraffin – fire all over the deck. Half-bricks sailing in on the breeze. Right through the porthole. And there was me, shot straight out of my paralysis and throwing myself on to one of them. Couldn't believe it was me. It must have been a genuine fit.

"I'd grabbed an oar or maybe it was one of Ron's wonderful fitted plank-seats. Sheer luck, but I knocked one of them straight into the canal. Then the Sisters all started pitching in. Luce turned one of them into a Black and White Minstrel with a tin of pitch. His mates probably repatriated him the next day.

"Meanwhile Ruth and Adrienne went for the enemy's Top Prick with a couple of theatrical scimitars – cardboard, but flashing like steel.

"That was it. We set sail on the evening tide. And I've been with them ever since. Not much of a performer on stage, though. I'm good at dumb animals, clockwork soldiers and the back legs of things. In street theatre it doesn't matter because you're all in it together.

"The Sisters got me writing things – bits and pieces. Short sketches, skits, daft histories. I did one on my days in the store, called *No Madam, We're Not Talking Crocodiles*. Lately I've done a lot on our Home Grown Shows."

"Home grown?" It had been Luke's first contribution, apart from listening, for the length of a pizza, apple pie and two pots of tea.

"Yes. Wherever the Siren Sisters go, we write a show based on the locality – the history, the scandals and intrigues, the personalities . . . We hold the mirror up to nature as the Bard neatly put it. So Badgerville had better watch out."

"I'll put round a warning."

"On the contrary, it's your help I'll be needing, because the Sisters will expect a script to come home to."

"You want me to rat on friends and neighbours?"

"It's not like that at all. You'll find we're not vicious, but full of fun – and love. You can just take me places, answer questions, fill in the details. A guide dog!"

"Thanks."

"You're welcome ... In return for your help, we'll give you a small jumping-on part. No, not walk-on. In street theatre nobody walks anywhere. You jump, do cartwheels, leap from great heights, crawl on hands and knees or simply get thrown on. But sure as eggs, you never walk."

Second tea-shop: the Norton had cruised to a halt and a fill-up at the motorway pumps. There was a short queue in the cafeteria. Petra relieved Luke of her rucksack and went to sit down. "Just tea, thanks," she said, having counted out the last of her money.

"You want something to eat, Don?" The stranger's voice made Luke swivel round, for it was a voice he had heard before, and not in happy circumstances: 'You want something to eat, Don?' It was the Belfast accent of two nights ago.

"Just coffee." And that was the Don voice, from behind the beams of the parked van: 'Stop it there, son!' Luke checked the turn of his head. Still looking for the fire-raiser? He decided he had had one encounter too many with Don and his friend. Fingers crossed they don't recognise me. Even if they do, so what? He ordered a pot of tea and stole another look at Don: tallish, around thirty, silvery-blond hair artificially waved, fair-faced, would pass for good-looking; like a model in a mail order catalogue. He was as smart as a model, wearing a green cord blouson, green flannels with razor-sharp creases and ankle-height sports shoes in red and white. He had gone to sit down three tables away.

"My driving couldn't have been that reckless, Luke." Petra had read his look of unease. "Or have I worn you out with my jabbering? If I go talking too much, just bop me."

"It's not that." Luke explained what had happened to him the other night on his way home from the badger sett. "Gave me a shock, that's all."

"Carrying guns?"

"Air rifle – something like that."

"And you weren't trespassing?" Her eyes travelled past Luke to watch the two men at the table behind him. "I mean, what could they have been guarding?"

Luke shrugged. He'd not given it much thought. "Up there, it's just hills and forest." He smiled. "Course, it could have been the rabbit droppings." His voice was an almost inaudible whisper. "I read in a magazine that certain rabbit droppings, if treated with a special chemical and then coated with sugar are . . ."

Petra's eyes had widened, gleaming with astonishment. "Rabbit droppings?"

"They bottle them and sell them as contraceptive pills to Third World countries."

"Idiot! Do you take the piss out of everybody you meet?"

"Only folks I like."

Petra stared at Don and his companion. "They're either cops in plain clothes or gangsters."

"The one with the shoulder-pads is Irish."

"Terrorists? I don't reckon so. Paddy's too cuddly . . . Hey, don't look round but they're using one of those walkie-talkies." She was so busy watching that she replaced her cup on the edge of the saucer and tea flooded over the table. "Sorry." They mopped up with serviettes. Before the job was finished, Don and Paddy were striding purposefully to the entrance. "He's practically all in green . . . Huh, the Green Knight!"

What Petra missed, but Luke noticed, was the attention Don and Paddy paid to her as they passed. Don even clicked his tongue.

"Close up, he's a bit like Steve McQueen."

"Steve McQueen's dead."

"Then a heated-up Steve McQueen."

Don and Paddy waited outside the café, staring across the deserted car park.

"We'd better not make a move till they've left," thought Luke and accepted another cup of tea from Petra.

"They're waiting for somebody. Using the walkie-talkie again . . . This is intriguing, Luke. Guns in the dead of night, secret rendezvous at motorway cafés – I thought you said life in Badgerville was dull?"

He was beginning to wonder if he'd been wise to open his mouth. I should have known: tell her an inch, she'll imagine a yard. On the other hand, this was a late hour to be playing verbal footsie on CB radio.

"There they go!" She was up, crossing towards the café window which overlooked the car park. All thoughts of a third cup of tea were forgotten. "That must be theirs – the Land Rover."

"Toyota Landcruiser."

"Good, Luke. You're entering into the spirit of things."

He had to admit it, he was as curious as she was. "Talking to a bloke in a . . . Lamborghini? Those are special."

"That's Italian – so how about the Mafia?"

Whatever its purpose, the meeting was soon over. The Lamborghini headed at speed for the motorway exit. "We'll never know. It's back to the horse and cab, Holmes."

But Petra held Luke on the spot. She pointed towards Don and Paddy who were now crossing to the lorry park. "Trucks, Luke."

"Two container lorries had pulled off the motorway; huge, high-sided jobs, six-wheeled. They answered Don's torch-signal with a flash of beam lights, slowed, and pulled up alongside the lorry park. Both drivers got down and shook hands warmly with Don and Paddy.

"That's it – he's their pilot. They're to follow the Landcruiser."

Luke observed, "There are no markings."

"Stolen trucks, maybe . . . This could be the beginning of my first front-page story."

The Landcruiser had pulled out in front of the trucks. Lights flashed. The convoy headed north.

"So that's that," said Luke resignedly.

"It damn well isn't, my dear Watson." Petra was crossing at a trot towards the Norton.

"But – "

"No buts – remember what Vera said. We're going to grab our horse and cab and tuck ourselves in behind." She grinned. "Our play's begun, Luke: Act One, Scene One – *Secret Cargoes!*"

The scissor-wind in Luke's face lost its cutting edge, yet it was too late for dozing. He had broken through the fatigue barrier. I'm so tired, I'm coming out the other side. In fact, he was feeling light-headed. Must be the whiff of grade-one Bolivian hash Pete suspects in those trucks.

On second thoughts, I'm probably dropping off: found, one corpse flattened into the concrete of the motorway. Youth of seventeen, appeared to be laughing insanely at time of decease. Brilliant future as paint-tin stamper, paper-boy and odd-job gardener cut short.

"Gardener at your age?"

"Why not? I like to landscape things . . . I've done a Japanese garden, just with raked gravel and a chunk of limestone. I've got ideas for rearranging the hills, and painting the dry-stone walls blood orange, or what Monarch calls Spanish Sunset."

He had almost written off the trucks, decided that Don and Paddy were probably not the men who had stopped him on the moor; after all, what did it matter if they were? It came as a surprise, then, to see the container trucks head off the motorway towards Rowmanton, nearest large town to Wynster Bridge. Petra was giving him an exaggerated head salute, the only meaning of which could be 'What did I tell you?'

At the traffic island there were three possible routes for the trucks to take: they selected Luke's route home. So what? I mean, so what? He was amazed how Petra had turned the most ordinary event into something dramatic; a fantasy. And what was just as surprising, this was the way Luke was beginning to perceive events. There's more happened to me in the last twenty-four hours than the whole summer put together.

Vera: 'Pete will be a tonic for the Waller household'. Thanks, Vera. Never a truer word; signed: two octogenarians in a geriatric ward.

There was still time for Petra's crime story to be re-routed as the convoy approached the end of a dual carriageway. There were two alternative plots: direct for Rowmanton or the hill-run for Wynster.

Don and Paddy in the Landcruiser elected for plot-line number two, and the pace of the trucks dropped to that of a camel train as one sheer climb seemed to surmount another; where hillcrest vied with hillcrest to be first at the stars.

Petra's natural impatience made her look to overtake, but the road narrowed. It did a convincing impersonation of the diabolical Corkscrew at Alton Towers where Dad once took Luke on a birthday treat.

They followed the convoy right to Wynster – or almost

right to it, for on the brow of the hill which eventually circled and dipped into the town, the trucks slowed to a halt; and so did Petra.

The Landcruiser had stopped ahead in a layby and signalled the trucks to pull in.

"What do we do?"

"Take cover, I think."

Petra didn't argue. She wheeled the Norton towards the open gate into a meadow. She took off her helmet. She said nothing, merely stared ahead of her. For a city girl, she's as alert as a fox. Fact is, with that hair, she looks like a fox. Well, maybe too cuddly for a fox.

They could hear nothing but the restless brush of the wind in a hawthorn over the dry-stone wall. The air smelt of charlock and mown grass.

"They seem to be waiting for somebody."

Luke reminded her: "You've got your headlamp on." Immediately she switched it off, but both sensed that they had been seen.

"It's a public road – I've paid my licence."

There was no time for debate. "They're coming!"

"Surely not -"

"For rabbit droppings? I doubt it. Come on." No time for a citizen's arrest and body search; and no stretching of the imagination required. Don and Paddy had emerged from the first truck and strode up past the tail-lights of the second. "Into the field, Pete."

"Like hell I will. This is a free . . ." She snatched another look at Don and Paddy. They were not checking tyre pressures. They were coming up the road. Paddy switched on a powerful torch.

Together, Luke and Petra dragged the Navigator into the meadow. Its wheels crackled over stubble. The ground was tilting. "Get on."

Luke found himself in the driver's seat, which made

it tricky for Petra to climb aboard because of the fat rucksack he still carried. Her feet trailed and she was never really astride as the Navigator quickened towards a copse of elms. They coasted over a bank of ferns and halted in the dark shelter of the trees.

They watched. The two men had entered the meadow. The torch was trained along the dry-stone wall and then out into space. "We were pushing our luck," murmured Luke, very scared. He was pleased – grateful even – that Petra did not try to brazen things out. She too was taken by surprise; shaken.

Her voice was soft, faraway: "Maybe they *are* criminals."

Luke was silent. They watched the darkness, expecting the torch beam to advance, but the men had already given up the search. A few moments later, the truck engines revved. They pulled away. "You know what, Luke?"

"What, Pete?"

"Those guys have cooked their goose."

He stopped himself from repeating the words. "Oh? Exactly how?"

"Because until this minute, it was all a bit of a lark, to pass the journey along – right?"

"If you say so."

"But they came after us. They stopped the whole convoy just for us."

Luke eased off Petra's rucksack. "Uncle Pete? Would you let me drive into town?"

"You think I'm fantasising?"

"I think that's a very long word for this time of night."

She settled him on the machine. "It suits you." Before climbing on the pillion, she paused. She leaned over the handlebars and kissed him. "I've felt like doing that ever since the Peace Camp. Okay?"

As so often happened when she was dead tired, Petra slipped into sleep and then emerged from it with her brain working overtime. Eyes wide, brain like a timebomb, she stared out of the window of the spare room at Church House into a sky so full of stars there seemed no space for darkness. The church clock spoke from nearby. She counted the chimes.

A day separated from the Sisters, and missing them deeply. This silence gives you earache. Two nights ago at this time, we were all together in the cell. Everybody panned to the world except Vera. Strange, there's no sense of her here, except for Luke and his dad waiting . . . waiting. Sad, really. They seem to be spending their lives going round in circles and don't realise it. It's a bit spooky – Alfred with his grand mural, trying to capture the beauties of Wynster before it decays from neglect or gets nuked into the next world; and Luke pouring his soul into strange gardens.

Petra gazed down at the garden beneath the rim of the moor. Beautiful – but weird: a flat oval of raked gravel; and in the centre, on a brick plinth, a slab of limestone about four feet high, slightly hollowed out and twisting towards the sky. Majestic yet agonised.

"Like this country," Luke had said.

In the light from an ancient lamppost at the corner of the garden, the raked pattern in the gravel seemed to connote a hidden language; an incantation.

"What does it mean, Luke?"

He had pretended not to understand. "Mean?"

"Is it a rune, a magic code?"

"Just a garden."

What am I letting myself in for? To me, that garden speaks of the impossible: a world without change. "If a leaf or a blossom fell on your neat gravel, Luke, would you remove it?"

42

He shook his head. "According to the book on Japanese gardens, a blossom is a sign."

"And a leaf?"

"You should ask Vera – she's the fortune-teller."

Petra had much preferred the flower garden on the higher level, where the moor took off in a sweeping curve. Here were things she could relate to – colour and mass and pattern, shaken by the hill wind. Perhaps this was the other side of Luke. "I don't know the names of flowers, except for roses and forget-me-nots. But I'd like to learn them. Same with birds and butterflies. Yes, I'd like to be up on such things."

That pleased Luke. Made his day, this strange boy with sea-blue eyes; a prisoner, Petra throught, in his own sad space. "You and your dad are the original Odd Couple," she had said.

"Like octogenarians in a geriatric ward?"

"You've noticed, then?"

"Vera's words."

Naturally.

Petra sat on a low chair in front of the wide-open window, and the moor seemed to swallow up both space and time. It's as though I've driven into a time warp. This house, for instance: built to last for ever, yet with every sign of falling to bits. The hottest summer on record, yet it smells damp. It's as if they've either just moved in or are just about to move out – all these patches on the walls where pictures used to be; the shape of a sideboard, vanished into its own pale outline.

She had commented on the bare stone floors. "You could film *Wuthering Heights* in here."

"Stone's our material round these parts. You ought to understand that, with a name like Petra."

"I was misnamed. I'm a brick person really. Brick's warm and colourful."

"Okay for southerners, maybe. Vera prefers brick."
Luke's eyes sparked. "That's because she and Dad are
chalk and cheese."

Something in that. Vera had not had much good to
say about her husband, the Reverend Alfred Waller. In
her report, he had come over as a wimp: full of fuss, like
an overflow pipe, so Vera put it. "In Wynster," she had
said, "Alfred's nicknamed the Red Reverend, because he's
a sucker for lost causes. While everybody else in the town
shouted hip-hip-hurrah for the Falklands War, Alfred did
the opposite. When the town tut-tutted over the Miners'
Strike, Alfred supported them to the hilt – and we got
petrol bombs in Church Hall."

"That sounds pretty impressive to me," Petra had replied.

"It's all talk, though, and no action. Fair words butter
no parsnips ... Oh, he's just ..." She had shrugged.
"Irritating. His other name is the Reverend Bumble."

What Vera had not thought to mention was Alfred's
appearance. "Your dad's the best-looking bloke I've seen in
ages," Petra had told Luke. "I bet a few of his parishioners
have fancied him over the years. I predict Ruthy will go
a bundle on him, even though he's Mr Scarecrow, all his
clothes hanging off him, and his grey hair turning that
baggy old suit into a dog's blanket."

"Don't tell him that," Luke had warned. "He'll only
think you're trying to cheer him up. Of course, if Vera
told him, then he'd be the cow that jumped over the moon."

Well, I like him. He's going into the play. Loveable,
that's for sure; unless you're on the receiving end of a
loveable archeological specimen. Vera just got tired of him.
But not Luke. He loves Alfred. Puts up with a lot too, I
guess.

Very patient with people, Luke – all those instructions
from old Miss Hillsmore this afternoon on what to do
and what not to do with her precious garden, snappy as

a Jack Russell, and yet not a word: "Yes, Connie – okay, Connie . . ." With me, a mite testy now and then; with Vera, well – he stayed pretty cool when she insisted on treating him like a turnip-head wrapped in a damp teatowel. Scared of her, is he? Alfred is.

"Luke needs budging." This had been Alfred's judgment on his son, as Luke had served a chicken dinner with roast potatoes and homegrown broccoli. "Too stuck in his ways."

"Which makes a pair of us, Dad."

Provoked, Alfred had launched into an account of how busy he was. "Carnival is going to be the biggest thing in these parts since the Norman invasion. Your Siren Sisters, Pete, will be only one top attraction among hundreds. There'll be twenty nations represented. At least fifty floats for the procession through the town. Eight bands, including a steel band from Birmingham, paying their own fares. There'll be balloon trips, tug-o'-war, a motorcycle stunt team, a folk-dance display, a troupe of mummers – wonderful! Local radio will be doing a spot on us and – who knows – we might even get featured on the box."

Alfred had paused. He looked gaunt, strained, decidedly overworked. If he was fifty, he ws beginning to look sixty, Petra thought. He had got up and crossed to the kitchen drawers. "You put all that effort in, and what happens? You get hate mail like this." He flicked open a letter. "I'll spare you the details. It says, if I want peace and quiet and a happy family life, I should cancel. Tell the blacks and the yellows and the reds – brackets, CND, it says here – to stay at home . . . How do you deal with warped minds like that?"

Alfred had looked to Luke for support. "Well?"

"Well what?"

"You know what I mean."

"I know you've had one mild heart attack, and you're going all out for the big one."

"You think we should quit?"

Luke had been slow to answer. He smiled; a smile tinged with doubts. "I've misplaced one parent. I don't want to be accused of carelessness by losing two."

"Nonsense. All this tension is keeping my adrenalin running."

"But in the end, what good will the Carnival do – what'll it change?"

"Will people have fun?"

"I suppose so."

"Then it's achieving something."

Petra had come in. "That's all the Siren Sisters ever expect to achieve, Luke. Songs and stuff don't change the world, but they keep people going."

Alfred had been intrigued by the idea of Petra writing a play about Wynster Bridge and its people. "A drama documentary? That means from this moment we're all actors on stage."

Luke said he wasn't sure it was a good idea to tell people. "You'll get everybody acting up, showing their best sides. Jostling about to create juicy parts for themselves. Dad will."

"Not at all," asserted Alfred, for the first time in many weeks noticing the grey hairs and dandruff on his suit and raising a hand to brush them off.

"You're at it already." Luke turned to Petra. "This is what he's been waiting for – Alfred, Prince of Wynster. Though with your bad ankle, Dad, you'd be more suited as Richard the Third with his club foot."

Alfred had shaken his head. "Do you know, Pete, the two people closest to me in the world are my harshest critics?"

Before Luke had fallen asleep, as easily and as completely as a well-oiled drawbridge, he had dwelt on the merits of the first girl in his life who could down a pint of cider without swallowing. "And every drop deserved," she had said. From Sunday lunchtime onwards she had toured the territory, with Luke as courier. "First, the town centre, then we'll work out in circles to the country districts."

"Doing what?"

"Talking to people, of course. Getting copy for the play." They had started in the pub garden of the Rising Sun on the stroke of twelve. In a large black leather notebook Petra jotted the reminiscences of Geoff Lord (called Lord Geoff), which poured as fluently as his ale. Geoff had played for Glasgow Rangers, then Rotherham, and been manager of Wynster Athletic when they got trounced eight nil in the Cup by Halifax. "When things like that happen, Pete, you either take to drink or make a profit out of it."

She had gone on to chat to Wynster's oldest inhabitants – at least those with strength enough to get up Hill Rise to order the usual. Ned Holden talked about the General Strike as if it were yesterday, yet thought today was Friday. Joe Chadwick had worked on Tattershall land for fifty years: they'd given him an electric kettle. "Trouble wor, I'd no electric."

Petra turned to Luke who had so far been cast in a non-speaking part. "Tattershall land?"

"Local squire. When the Enclosures came, the Tattershalls could afford the fences. Colonel Richard Prynge Tattershall is our MP."

From the Rising Sun Petra's net spread to meet Irwin Turner, the last cobbler this side of the Pennines to make clogs; to look around the workshop of Ken Jowett, a craftsman in church furniture whom Luke helped with sanding and occasional jobs on the lathe; to meet Wynster's only recorded artist, a watercolourist called Landseer B. Davies who doubled up as a piano tuner and market gardener. "Luke here is your real artist, Pete. He's more than a damn good gardener – he's a landscapist, like Capability Brown."

In her notebook Petra had scribbled 'Capability Waller'.

Among others qualifying, in Luke's judgment, as the town's local colour, was Mr Innocence, his old rural studies teacher and mentor in the country code. "Mr Innocence?"

"That's because he'd start every other sentence with 'In a sense'. The cuts-people forced him into early retirement."

It had turned out an unwelcome visit. Mr Innocence had withdrawn from the world. Behind shut curtains he watched videos all day. His cottage was a shambles. They had caught him in the middle of *Gone With the Wind*, which Mr Innocence said he had seen a hundred times. "Which is about half the times I've seen *Citizen Kane*."

After they had departed, without being offered tea and with Mr Innocence showing no inclination to exercise the pause button, Petra had commented. "There are plenty of folk round here with their blinds closed, Luke."

"With what's going on in the world, do you blame them?"

"Don't you?"

Luke was not sure which he admired more, Petra's seemingly tireless energy or the ease with which she got on with people (Mr Innocence excepted). There are people talking to me, calling me Luke, who've never bothered to give me the time of day till now.

He was not ungrateful: reflected glory's better than none at all.

At some time or another during their afternoon and evening chats with the locals, Petra remembered to drop in the question, "Have you noticed any unusually large cargoes passing to and fro lately?" The answers were always

48

in the negative. "It must have been ghosts we followed last night, Luke."

He had nodded, preferring it that way. Yet when he fell asleep, when he dreamed, he was unable to banish the ghosts as effortlessly as his waking mind had done. Where had Don and his trucks vanished to?

It was a dream of being trapped: open country, yet all the roads in blind darkness were blocked. He was riding out of the meadow with Pete. The entrance gate was barred. He was walking her up to the badger sett. The track was blocked.

"Stop it there, son!" He raised his eyes from the knife-sharp crease of green trousers to the green blouson, and saw Steve McQueen. He felt, in the dream, immense relief. Steve McQueen's dead. This is only a dream.

Petra's voice sprang from behind him; just her voice, for she was not visible in the dark:

"I know who you are!"

Luke saw the gun. He heard himself call out, "Don't shoot!"

He awoke, and the sweat was cold on him.

Chapter 3

Luke needn't have been so anxious. The Steve McQueen look-alike had already journeyed south. "Sorry to have dragged you all this way, Don. But it's the company rule on matters of high security – nothing through the post and definitely no phone calls. This country's bugged from Land's End to John O'Groats."

"That's fine by me, Mr Rhodes. Wynster is Deadsville. It's nice to get back to the bright lights."

"Excellent. Deadsville is why we chose the town." Rhodes was studious grey: granite head topped with grey; grey-suited, with a single blue stripe down a grey silk tie. "Softly-softly, Don."

He had slender white hands which rested motionless on a pink blotter with leather corners, gilt-embossed, initialled LDR. His office was the ultimate in high-tech design – plastic, aluminium, straight lines, plush carpet in wine red.

On the wall behind him – where only his guests could see it – was a nineteenth-century painting of a young girl bathing naked in a river. "You like the picture, Don? It's an original William Etty."

Don Neeson considered it soft porn, but did not say so. "Very skilfully executed, sir."

"Professional. A quality I admire above all things . . . She's rather too young for both of us, I fear."

"She looks pretty well developed from here."

Rhodes sighed. "It reminds me, Don, not to grow old too quickly." He stood up and crossed to the window. "From the twelfth floor, London doesn't look at all the garbage city it is on the ground. Quite beautiful, in fact."

"If you've a head for heights."

"Which I'm assured you have, Don. Among many other virtues."

"I appreciate the chance you've offered me, Mr Rhodes."

"We recruited you *because* of your record, Don, not in spite of it. Where did you serve exactly – Africa, mainly, wasn't it?"

"Got my training as you know from the Koevoet in Namibia. Tough and – "

"Professional."

"Oh yes. But the world's been my oyster since then."

"You were with the Contras in Nicaragua?"

"Contras? CIA, Mr Rhodes."

"Where you got shot up for your pains?"

"Nine months in hospital, sir."

"Then you'll be glad to be back in action – even if it's a silence job in Deadsville?"

Don nodded. "The hunting's good – plenty of foxes and pheasants."

"Great." Hurriedly now, Rhodes glanced at his watch. "From this point onwards, Don, things will be especially delicate. The first shipment has been a success. We've got the right staff and proper protection. Soon the company will have a reasonable return for a very substantial investment." He raised a finger to his lips. "So, to repeat the words from on high, softly-softly all the way. No publicity. We can do with that like a dose of bubonic plague – right?

"You and your crowd should enjoy yourselves as much as possible within that rule. The less you talk to the natives, the better. Don't drink in the local pubs – go over to . . . Where's the nearest big town?"

"Rowmanton."

"Fine. Shake a leg over there. We'll pay for weekends

down in the smoke once they've served guard for six months."

"Thanks, Mr Rhodes – they'll appreciate that bit of news."

Rhodes slid open a desk drawer and removed a package. "All your instructions are in here, Don. Don't leave the documents around. Tell your people as little as possible. Pay them, feed them, booze them up – and shut them up." Don was almost at the door when Rhodes added, "I forgot to ask, Don – any worries at all – no incidents?"

"Nothing to speak of, Mr Rhodes."

Rhodes spotted the hesitation. "But something?"

"Not really worth mentioning . . . It's just that on the run in, I thought we were being tailed."

"Followed? Not to the . . . ?"

"Turned out to be just a couple of kids on a motorcycle, sir."

Rhodes pressed back in his chair, relieved. "You had the old ticker palpitating then, Don." He traced the blue line of his silk tie. "If all we've got to fear is a couple of kids on a motorcycle, we'll be okay – right?"

"Right, Mr Rhodes."

What Petra guessed must be a lizard, or even a small crocodile, was about to head up Luke's trouser leg. In normal circumstances she would have warned him, but he had been so starchy about her voice carrying up wind and frightening off the badgers, that she had kept silent.

She had packed a fortnight into one day, and had talked incessantly since she had arrived at Monarch to pick up Luke after work. She had caused a small sensation by circling the mill yard at hooter time, dressed in green shorts with a white stripe and a yellow sweater emblazoned with THE SIREN SISTERS on the front and DON'T PANIC on the back.

"Lady bleeding Godiva on a motorcycle!" Madge had called to Luke, who had been helping Grizzly Gifford in Stores and listening to his usual dirge upon the State of the Nation (bad) and Youth's Attitude to Their Elders (even worse). "Come and feast your eyes, Luke."

Petra had halted astride the Navigator and gazed up at five storeys of summer-lit windows. And five storeys of summer-lit windows gazed down at her. A chorus of enquiries fizzed out from Maintenance, from Packaging, from the Boiler Room, even from the offices where the view was partially blocked by the managing director's vintage Bentley.

"What do you want, love?" Madge's voice climbed above the rest.

"Oh, everybody," called Petra. "I'm leafleting for one of the best touring shows on the road." She reached back to the panniers over the rear wheel. "My friend Luke's in there. He's helping me."

"Hey, pet!" A voice boomed from the fifth floor. "What's a spotty schoolkid doing riding a British Masterpiece? You're too young for a sugar daddy."

From a window below, "How about a quick leg-over love?"

Petra answered boom with boom: "It's not the mating season for Nortons, friend. If you're on heat, try a Yamaha!"

Laughter.

Luke queued for his own leaflet declaring the Siren Sisters to be 'the liveliest community theatre on land or water'. Standing in line was a small price to pay for getting close to the one woman within five hundred yards dressed as though life was something to be enjoyed.

"We're going to do a lunchtime gig on this spot," Petra told Luke.

He had been very doubtful. "The boss won't even

let us have our bait on the grass, so you'd never – "

"It's all arranged. I talked to His Nibs this morning. Delighted, he said. But no politics. He's promised a tenner for the kitty and we can pass round the hat."

Luke had expected to be driven home. Instead, "I've brought a picnic. Where can we go and swim? In the open – and no chlorine."

"I've no costume."

"Neither have I." Over the wrought-iron bridge which gave Wynster its name; along a lake-like stretch of river beside a frieze of parkland spruce, where a bronze-domed bandstand watched its own reflection; past stone cottages above white-water cascades that divided the calm from the turbulent at Ecclestone's red-brick mill; then on from the weir to where the river became an olive green and sky-speckled serpent beneath the trees.

"I've so much to tell you, Luke."

Sycamore on water duty. Pillars of light, pools of light, the Navigator steep-climbing, then dipping once more, turning the trees into rhythms of burnt umber and flashes of blue; Luke's country, each moment taking him farther from the tongue-tied imbecile of Saturday at the court and the Peace Camp, towards a person he recognised; a person he could live with.

They stopped under an arcade of leaves, silent. She followed his pointing finger. "Remind me what I'm supposed to be looking at."

"Past the willows – see now?"

"Something with wings?"

"You said you wanted to learn the names of things . . . Fieldfare. Smaller than a mistle thrush, larger than the song thrush."

Now she saw it. She was pleased, even though she suspected Luke of flaunting his knowledge. "But not quite as rotund as a skippertail?"

"Skippertail?"

"Flies in from the Azores perched on the back of a male swallow. Departs for southern climes every Shrove Tuesday."

"Rabbit droppings to you!" Luke got off the Navigator. He looked towards the river, half in brown shadow, half in sunlight. "By the way, the Wynster is the only river in the country stocked with cold-water piranha."

Petra did not seem to be bothered at the prospect of flesh-eaters in her bath water. She leapt down the bank and landed on a huge, sunny bolder. "Don't turn your back," she called, beginning to strip off. "I want your honest opinion."

As they often do in books, Luke gulped. She was going in naked; and what a summer this had been to dye her so brown, save for the white bikini shape left on her buttocks. He was mindful of what Madge had been saying on Friday about what was permitted on Friday nights. This was Monday – would Madge approve?

"Opinion?"

"There." She stood where the trees had granted the sun an unbroken view of the earth. "Am I or am I not dumpy?"

Afterwards they climbed a winding path from woods into high meadows. They ate their picnic and waited for dusk. "What's so wonderful about badgers?"

"You'll see . . . but we'll need some hush."

She had told him about her day: about signing on the dole and using Alfred's address; about leafleting, persuading shopkeepers to put up Siren Sister posters – and about Mrs Fowles at the corner store. "She remembers Steve McQueen . . . so we've tracked our Don down at last, to two boxes of groceries. He seems to have a soft spot for jam doughnuts and Dutch cigars."

55

"What did she say about him?"

"That he was a very polite-mannered young man. Always puts something in the cancer box. First appeared about six weeks ago."

"I reckon you'll have to find somebody else to play the wicked Sheriff of Nottingham."

"You think so?" Petra said she was not giving up on Don that easily. "These days villains don't go round with black moustaches and steel hooks hidden up their sleeves. If they're to be good villains, they've to be charming. And Don's charming."

"You said Alfred was charming."

"True." This had silenced her, which was as well, for the badgers were beginning to stir.

They were in the middle of an oak wood. Grass banks had been sliced from the lower ground, leaving walls of limestone that formed a dell strewn with holly and gorse.

"Look!" A tremor; a darkening at the mouth of the sett beneath a grassy overhang: a snout; one nose sniffing at the twilight. "It's coming." Luke was electrified. She had not seen him like this: his lazy, laid-back manner was gone. He quivered in the dusk like the badger.

Petra followed his gaze and caught something of his excitement. Yes: one snout and slowly, slowly one head of black and white fur. No audience ever awaited the arrival of performers on stage with greater eagerness or intensity.

Out came the head; paused.

"Can it see us?"

"Badgers are shortsighted. We're down wind so they'll not get a scent of us. Often I go right on to the bank – when the wind's right. I've been six feet off them . . . there comes the female."

The male badger was out in the open now, scratching himself as though the fresh air felt more irritating than fleas.

"Two more!"

"Cubs ... The female's having a scratch too. You'd think they were ripping their hide to pieces."

Petra, the town girl, had seen nothing like this – a whole badger family romping, wrestling, chasing; not just the cubs but the parents, pitching in with relish. "Are they really playing?"

"They love it. Carnivores, you see."

"Carnivores?"

"Flesh-eaters ... They've the time to spend their energies on play, whereas herbivores, grass-eaters, have got to keep on eating their own weight in greens to keep alive ... The shrew, for instance – he's an insectivore – has to eat half his own weight every twenty-four hours to stay alive."

"Mr Badger in *The Wind in the Willows* used to brew tea and smoke a pipe – do they?"

Luke was thinking of a suitable reply, when the badger family abruptly ceased their play; for a moment froze, then bolted for the sett.

"What happened?"

Like the badgers, Luke twitched his nose in the wind. "Not us, I don't think."

Petra cupped an ear. "Listen!" They held breath, stared along the wall of the dell into a screen of silver birch. "Hear that?"

"Tractors?" He thought again. "Too dark."

"Heavy vehicles, Luke. And not far off."

Can't be. Beyond these woods was a brief stretch of moorland, then forest. "Going where?"

Petra was up and running towards the sound which had sent the badgers into hiding. Luke followed. No option. Last year's leaves, rolled into deep corners of the dell, scattered as they raced up the winding path. A single, long meadow separated woods of oak and silver birch from the first of the forest pines. They were rewarded for their haste. "Two trucks, Luke." Disappearing among the firs along a forest track. "Like Saturdays night . . . Well, Mr Bloodhound, this is your country – where are they heading?"

"Furmiston Forest."

"Why?"

"I've not the slightest." He shook his head, stumped. "Not really my territory. It's all black forest, pines planted nose to tail in endless lines."

"Big is it, the forest?"

"Stretches for miles. Kind of forbidden ground, actually – what with the old leadmines. Very dangerous."

"Maybe there's a sudden demand for lead."

"That'd be good news for Dad. It'll make a change from having the stuff nicked from the church roof . . . But not possible. The mines haven't operated this fifty years."

"Come on, I'm curious." His legs were longer, but hers were faster. She thought better of racing him through the brambles. "Hold!" She thrust out her hand for his and they picked a careful route down through brambles, nature's barbed wire, towards the forest track.

"See," whispered Luke, watcher of the skies, "Barn owl!"

"White."

"Beautiful."

"Ghostly in this light . . . Who owns those leadmines?"

"Forestry Commission, I think." He wasn't happy. It was years since he'd wandered in these parts with his friend, Chiuni. They'd put the wind up each other with wild tales; eventually their nerve had snapped and they'd done a four-minute mile out of there and never gone back.

"Scared?" She missed nothing. They were almost at the track. In the twilight, they could scarcely see more than a yard ahead.

"Of course not. It's just that this place has bad vibes."

She gripped his hand. "If there's any place left in this world for werewolves, this is it." She gave a whoop. "There's one now!"

Luke missed his footing and stumbled into the dry ditch running alongside the forest track. "Nettles!" He rose, rubbing himself. "I'll need dock leaves."

"Walking wounded, follow me."

"What's the point?"

"I want to know how far it goes."

"Halfway in and halfway out." He was forced to follow her, at a rapid jog. Since he'd left school, since he'd given up the rock climbing, he was out of condition, despite all the garden-digging.

"What makes you so fit?"

"I told you – leaping on and off stage. Humping stage-props."

The track of grass and dry mud took a sharp curve. Immediately ahead of them were the trucks they had heard, tail-lights burning in the darkness, beams illuminating clouds of moths – and something that astounded Luke.

"Steel gates – a fence!" He couldn't believe it. The truck lights turned Furmiston into a stage, and the dominant stage-prop was a twelve foot steel-mesh fence topped with barbed wire. The double gates had been pegged back. They too were crowned with repeated strands of barbed wire. "There was never a fence."

The man who had pegged back the gates wore a combat jacket, of green and tan camouflage; and he carried a rifle across his shoulder.

"Armed guards? This isn't happening."

The thick butt of the rifle caught the light, and so did the smooth black telescopic sight on the barrel. "Are those legal?"

Luke appreciated the fact that Petra was not as cocky as she had been. "Who's checking?" She had not needed any persuading to take cover among the pines. "You want to get a bit closer?"

It was Petra's turn to brave things out. "Why not?"

He heard himself repeating, "How could there be a fence? There was never a fence."

The trucks had been waved forward through the gates. "You mean to say you didn't know about all this?" The truck drivers acknowledged the guard with a flash of their lights, then plunged down the pine-pillared avenue ahead of them. "You Wynster folk walk around in a dream."

All Luke could think of saying was, "There was never a fence. People used to walk . . . freely through there. It was only the mineshaft that had warning notices."

"Well in future they'll be needing passports."

They watched the guard lock the gates. He stared out for a few moments as if suspecting the hidden presence of strangers. He lit a cigarette. Behind him was a substantial wooden cabin, recently erected, with a chimney in the sloped roof, a stack of firewood outside and fire-fighting equipment along the rear wall.

"Here to stay."

"I reckon that's razor wire . . . Would you believe it – the Peace Camp, now this. He's even got a TV aerial."

"More like a transmitter," thought Luke.

"And you said I was imagining things, Luke Waller." The guard had strolled back to the hut, prompting Petra and Luke to approach the fence as if to prove that it was not a forest mirage. She touched the steel mesh. "It's real. But what the hell's going on through there?" She was pleased. "Our play's taking shape nicely. I've got plenty of characters, lots of background but until now – no story."

Luke felt Petra staring at him. He waited. She waited longer, still staring. He knew he would have to speak.

"What you're saying, if I'm not mistaken, is that your story . . ." He pointed through the fence. "Is in there?" She was closer to him, touching, still staring, urging his thoughts on. "And we've somehow . . . to go in there to get it?"

"We'll be needing wire-clippers," she said.

"Ah, the Unapproachable Norton, eh?"

Petra glanced up from polishing the Navigator's front hub and wheel chrome. "You know something about Nortons, Alfred?"

"As the old advert used to say. 'The Unapproachable Norton Long Stroke . . . The Norton *never* breaks valves'."

"Talking of never, I'd never have dreamed a minister would be a biker." It was as surpising as his thick northern r's and clipped a's.

"Once upon a time. I let Luke have my Suzuki GT 350, then alas we had to sell her. Went to a good home though."

Petra commiserated. "It must have been a wrench . . . All my family's had bikes of one sort or another. My eldest brother Tom – he's in Canada now – actually drove an Ajay racer of 1914 for a while. My dad's pride and joy was his 1950 Ajay 7R – "

"The Boys' Racer? Marvellous. I used to pray to the Almighty for a Matchless, the G3C Trials machine."

"And did the Almighty answer the prayer of one of his servants?"

"Afraid he didn't. On the grounds, I imagine, that motorcycles could put donkeys out of business."

"You want a ride, Reverend?"

Alfred cocked a leg over the machine, placing his hands on the grips. "Superb." He shook his head. "But I'm past it . . . the pushbike's too fast for me these days." He asked Petra how the play was going, and

61

she asked him what he knew about Furmiston Forest.

He mentioned the dangerous mineshaft. There had been a couple of tragic falls there in recent years, but he was as surprised as Luke had been to learn of the fence which now surrounded the forest. He had shrugged, "Still, I suppose that's to be expected when things go private."

"Then it's no longer Forestry Commission land?"

"Not for quite a while."

"Who owns land around it or nearby?"

"The Tattershalls, I guess – who else?"

"He's your MP, isn't he?"

"Colonel Tattershall, yes. Strong on law and order."

"Do you know him well enough to fix me an interview?"

"We've exchanged words once in five years, Pete. To say we don't see eye to eye is to put it mildly. A testimonial from me would bolt his door to you for ever. To be fair, though, there are plenty who consider Tattershall an excellent constituency MP."

"There are two other things I'd like to ask you, Alfred."

"Ask away."

"In this day and age, do you really believe in God?"

"I believe in God's Word."

"That's not answering the question."

"Isn't it?"

"You know it isn't. A divine being is one thing, teaching about how you should conduct your life is another . . . Vera lost her faith, didn't she – in God, I mean?"

Alfred was embarrassed and confused. He glanced at the time, forgetting that he no longer possessed a watch. "What was the other question?"

"Why is Vera so resentful of Luke?"

"Did Luke tell you she was?"

"No. It's just as plain as the nose on your face."

Alfred raised his defences. "Not true." How this girl asked questions; shot them like arrows. They were honestly meant so it was difficult to resent them. Yet they were too painful to cope with for long. "I'll leave you to your polishing."

Petra watched Alfred go, still limping, back to his beloved mural before starting his round of the parish. She thought, "They say northerners are supposed to be more open and frank. Where's the evidence?" And she warned herself, "One of these days you'll ask a question too many and get your block knocked off, so help you!"

Questions had been all the rage at Monarch Paints that morning, and every one of them was directed at Luke Waller, whom Madge addressed as 'Superstud'. The subject of the questions from Madge, Ellen, Freda and numerous other callers to the Filling Section, was Petra: where's she from? How old is she? Is that hair real? Where's she staying? Is there a lock on her door?

Have you kissed her yet?

Luke would have dearly preferred to be left alone with his thoughts. His mind was split between two sets of images, one in glorious Technicolor, the other in sombre black and white. The first was of Petra in the river, floating on her back among sprigs of green and fallen leaves: "Bring all your girlfriends here, do you?" And of her saying, copper flattened on floating head, eyes glittering, "Did anyone ever tell you – you've a beautiful body?"

He wanted to fix the moments so they would last for ever, yet he had to combat the second set of images – of trucks carrying mysterious cargoes through steel-mesh gates in the dead of night.

His workmates had somehow learnt of the play Petra was writing. Their questions were like wasps hustling for jam until he was forced to shift himself and do what Petra had asked of him – to find out about Furmiston.

"Good screwing country," asserted Ellen, but the others were a blank.

"Keep out of there, Luke," warned foreman Bill Gordon. "Those mineshafts are some of the deepest in the country. Run for miles. Treacherous."

Luke thought to ask, "Which way do they stretch – away from Wynster?"

"Every which way. I read they'd stopped diggin' when the church tower started to sag. One day, come a fortnight's heavy rain – and you know what? We'll disappear down one of them shafts."

"Aye," chipped in Madge, "and they'll write ghost stories about us – Wynster, the Vanished Village."

Luke asked Bill why people should want to put a twelve foot high fence round Furmiston, and Bill replied it was "A bloody good thing if it keeps kids out".

On the tip of Luke's tongue were the words, "And is it a good thing to drive ten ton trucks up there, and have guards carrying rifles with telescopic sights?" Yet he chose to say nothing. It would all sound a cock-and-bull story, the kind theatre people dream up to keep audiences amused.

"It's only common sense," said Bill. "Am I right?"

Luke nodded. "Common sense, Bill."

"I'm sorry, but you can't go in there – stop!"

Petra darted through a glass-panelled door past the secretary to the editor of the weekly *Rowmanton and Wynster Messenger* into a fug of pipe smoke and the smell of egg sandwiches. "I've a headline story, sir. And please excuse this haste."

Oliver Startup kicked back his swivel chair on castors. "Not today, thank you, whatever you're selling." He was big, bald and bored.

"I'm not selling," replied Petra holding up her leatherex diary. "I'm on to something – but I need information."

Startup squeaked; it was either him or one of the castors on his chair. "You've got a story – but we've got the information?" He launched a superior and withering smile. "It's all right, Mrs Phillips," he instructed his secretary. "I shall handle this little curiosity. Just keep the door ajar."

The editor had been in the middle of the *Daily Telegraph* crossword. He waved Petra into a specially low chair without castors, reserved for cub reporters who had got somebody's initials wrong or forgotten to use the paper's house style. "Do you do crosswords, Miss, er?"

"Petra Scales, and I'm afraid I've too much on my plate at present -"

"Seven letters, beginning with E. The clue is 'clever but not dynamite'."

"ERUDITE. Now if you'll hear me out, please."

Startup filled in the word approvingly. "I take it you weren't educated in these parts." He raised a hand as she tried to go on. "Let me guess, young lady – you've heard there's a yodelling cat trapped in some parish church belfry and you want us to finance the ladder? Or better still, you want us to sponsor you in the World Underwater Spaghetti Eating Competition? Let Mrs Phillips have the details on your way out."

Petra told herself, "Stay cool," but the words came out sharply. "My story may not be as erudite as those things, but it's quite possibly dynamite. First question: why is there a twelve foot fence round Furmiston Forest? Second, what's being shifted in there in vast trucks after dark? Third, what's your sitting MP Colonel Tattershall got to do with this business? And finally, where's his racing-driver son Lance come into it all?"

The effect of these questions on the editor of the *Messenger* was definitely more dynamite than erudite. He had been half up from his chair, leaning forward on his hands, head shimmering under the striplight directly above him. His mood was transformed. "Mrs Phillips, this person is leaving!"

"At least let me look through back copies of your paper."

"Sorry – absolutely pressing appointment. Cast a shadow in these premises again, Miss Scholes – "

"Scales!"

"Scales or Scholes, I'll have you for loitering and criminal trespass."

"Then there *is* something?"

"Out! and don't slam the – "

Petra did slam the door, so hard it opened again. "You've not heard the last of me, Mister."

She was followed, toe to heel, by Mrs Phillips who, once the editor's door was truly shut, seemed to be highly amused. "I think you ought to know," she said as Petra stepped into the dazzling hot High Street of Rowmanton, "that our little paper is actually owned by the Tattershalls. People call it *Tattershall's Tales*." It was woman to woman for a moment. "Why not try the library for back copies, and local radio if you want some action?"

Petra fished in her blouse pocket. "Here, Mrs Phillips. Two complimentaries for any Siren Sisters production." She grinned. "Look out for us in the local paper."

"What is it called?"

"The Mellport Stone. But Dad and me have another name for it – the Frost Demon."

"It's scary."

Petra had been in a bad mood when they met, and at her request Luke had brought her to a place of peace and quiet high in the moors.

"All sacred places are scary."

A crescent-shaped cliff of limestone formed a natural

amphitheatre. In the centre stood a gritstone rockstack over thirty feet high. She was impressed. "Definitely a giant. It's as if he's on stage, addressing his audience." She pointed at the nearly vertical cliff-face. "Is it where the townsfolk throw off sacrificial victims? Hell, what a drop!"

Beyond the Frost Demon the land rippled away into wheatfields interspersed with pastureland, then climbed again towards the green hump of the Winter Hill and the black-rock profile of Mellport Tor to the east. Patterns of green and gold were tinctured with poppy.

"Come and touch the rock."

"Not if it bites."

"That's the point. It bites if you don't touch it."

Her dark mood had faded. She paused at the top of the cliff and gazed at the sun rolling down the shoulder of Mellport Tor. "I'm welcome here," she said. "I can feel it."

Ahead of her on the sheer but not precipitous descent, Luke stopped and broke off a fragment of rock. "Look, Mother Nature's jewellery." He chipped out flakes of crystal with his fingernail. "Satin spar, they used to mine it."

She examined it in her palm, then slipped it into her pocket. "My jewellery, then."

From ground level, the gritstone Demon seemed to lunge at the sky. "I see what you mean, Luke – he's struggling to be free."

"Can you find a part for him in your play, Pete?"

"Looks a bit of a hammy actor to me. Perhaps a walk-on-and-fall-over part. Who made him?"

Luke said people thought the rock was a Bronze Age calendar stone. "Like Stonehenge."

"So there were Druids here?"

"Maybe . . . At Winter Solstice, the sun would touch

the pinnacle at dawn, and the priests would build fires behind the rock. Dad and me once dug a foot down and found some ash."

"But what did it mean – solstice?"

"The change of the year, from summer to winter. People were superstitious of change."

"Like the folks of Wynster today?" She prowled round the rock. "He looks very violent and destructive, this Frost Demon. I suppose you've to touch him to stop him coming to life."

Luke nodded. "With the tips of your fingers."

"I'd be tempted to lay off and see what happened."

"He's got another name – Devil's Needle, from the time of the Enclosures. The Devil would come at night and stitch up the countryside. In the morning . . ." He broke off, stared at Petra as the story took on a new meaning in his mind. "The people would find the land stitched up – with fences."

"Then there's a starring role for him after all. Still, I'd rather he came to life in the play than for real." She pressed her hand hard against the Demon. They sat together at the foot of the stone, full in the sun. "The Sisters do a play about death and resurrection, Luke. Must be very ancient, like your rock . . . St George is the comic turn. He gets into a swordfight with the King of Egypt – don't ask me why; and poor old Georgie Porgy is struck down dead. Everybody mourns. Buckets of tears slopped all over the place, much gnashing of teeth – we have a special teeth-clacking machine which Ron made. Then in comes Father Christmas and says, 'Rise up, bold fellow and fight again'. Which he does. Like the spring, the new year."

She suddenly pulled up her legs and rested her head on her knees. "What a pointless day it's been . . . I've got nowhere. All doors are slammed in my face and I probably deserve it. I've offended your dad. I've taken Vera's name in vain. I've been kicked out of the *Messenger* office. Everywhere, I've drawn a blank. The only guy who's shown a beetle turd's worth of interest is Len Williams at BBC Radio, and that was only because he fancied me.

" 'Come back when you've got evidence', they say."

Luke confessed that he too had drawn a blank. "We could forget it," he said. "Try a new tack."

"Forget it?" She leapt up. "Like hell I will." She stood over Luke. "Listen!" She finger-jabbed the air, reminding him of Vera. "I'm not just looking for a good plot for the play. I'm convinced there's something going on up there. And I'm going to find out, with or without your help."

Luke rolled out of her shadow and sprang up like the King of Egypt about to deliver St George a mortal wound. "You need me."

"I need nobody. Never have!" She stepped forward and fell flat over a stone.

He fought to keep his face straight, but the laughter surged up through him like boiling milk. The words danced ahead of him, "Rise up, bold fellow and fight again!" He helped her up and she slipped her arms round him. "Oh blow it!" She was crying and laughing at the same time.

Luke reached into his zip jacket. "Father Christmas got his dates wrong, sent these for you." He held a pair of wire-cutters in front of her wet eyes. "Are we still in business?"

"There was a young lady asking after you, Mr Neeson," said Mrs Fowles at Hilltop Stores, as Don Neeson called for three large boxes of groceries.

"Oh yes? By name?"

"No, just enquiring, like. You being a stranger in these parts. Course, she's a stranger too."

Don's face expressed disinterest, yet he stayed to talk. "I'm not sure if I know her."

"Oh, you'd recognise her – bright as a new pin, with red hair. Real tomboy type. Rides a motorbike."

"What was she wanting to know exactly?"

Mrs Fowles laughed. "She's not the only one – what's going on up at Furmiston?"

"Private contract, Mrs Fowles. We're not bothering the neighbourhood, are we?"

"Not at all." Her eyes lighted on the groceries. "Glad to have the extra custom." Mrs Fowles held the door open as Don loaded the Landcruiser. "Them clouds are welcome – this heat's killing me."

He scrutinised the sky with a shake of his head. "I'm the other way round. The more sun I get, the more I want." He paused. "This young lady, Mrs Fowles, is she staying locally?"

"Up at the Red Reverend's – that's what we call him on account of the opinions as land him in trouble. But he's kind and generous as the day is long. The lass is a friend of Luke's, the Reverend's boy."

"Up the road, you say?"

"Aye, Church House, what's left of it, them selling off their furniture and all."

"The girl – a student, is she?"

"The way she talks, I reckon she's a reporter." Mrs Fowles indicated the bright poster in her front window, advertising the Siren Sisters. "That's her thing too. They're putting on a show at Mr Waller's Grand Carnival next week . . . And to tell you the truth, Mr Neeson, not everybody's happy about being invaded by thousands of visitors."

"Thousands?"

"Well, likely hundreds, but who knows what mischief they'll get up to?"

Don Neeson climbed into his vehicle. "Thanks a lot, Mrs Fowles." And it was not only the groceries he had in mind.

Chapter 4

They rested the Navigator on its side under pines, and covered it with bracken. "Check!"

"Check?"

"Check gear."

"Oh . . ." I think she's decided we're in a war movie. The Dirty Duo.

"One pair wire-cutters."

"One pair wire-cutters."

She unzipped her shoulder bag. "One third-hand Minolta 35mm camera given me on my sixteenth by sister Lena; last owner, her husband Sam."

"You want me to repeat that?"

"Plus one long-throw lens to capture the blackheads on Demon Don's nose . . . So what have you brought?"

"Check: one Taiwan torch. One pair binoculars, made in Hong Kong. Fourth-hand, in exchange with Doug at the chip shop for Dad's exercise bicycle. Two Twix bars. And this." He held out a pine cone. "If all else fails, we squeeze the cone and disappear."

They paused at the fence, staying in the shadow of the pines. The sun was almost gone and the forest was a darkening cobweb of blue light. They did not speak – for they had gone through all the arguments. They held the clippers together: a ceremony. "Straight down and we'll bend it in from the bottom."

"Vera would be proud of you."

It pleased him, but he did not answer. "Here goes, then." As the steel-mesh was severed, he thought "Criminal damage" and pictured Dad's face. The gap opened wide enough to admit head and shoulders. Petra went through first and pulled Luke behind her. They pressed the wire back into place. From a distance it would look normal.

"We need to mark the spot in case we're in a rush." He snapped off a low branch and leaned it against a pine trunk opposite.

"But we'll be coming back in the dark."

He hadn't thought of that. He picked up the branch and stuck it in the fence. "We'll have to feel our way."

"And if there's an inspection?"

"We use the pine cone."

They plunged into the snare of brambles. "Good thing we decided on wellies." The firs grew in tight rows, creaking, head-rubbing. The odour of pine hung between the trunks, sweet and thick as cough mixture.

"Not impressed," decided Petra. "Reminds me of an underground car park." At least there was a soft welcome under foot. "How long before these pine needles turn to coal, Luke?"

"As long as it'd take to grow another Frost Demon."

Ahead, the trees divided to form a fire-break. This sloped towards the centre track, the route of the trucks. The sun had dropped through the pines on the opposite ridge. Its crimson fire now spilled out among the routes like a furnace overflowing. They followed the course of the track, keeping well within the line of the firs.

They stopped: crossroads. "Which way?"

"The old mineshafts are straight ahead."

"And so are the tyre marks." They edged out from cover. "Remember your Green Cross Code, Luke." They padded across rutted mud, over dog-tooth tread marks into the relief of shadow. "My God, what's that?"

They had seen the trapped squirrel simultaneously and stepped away into the light to avoid it. The squirrel's head was almost severed from its body by the steel trap. "It's dead, Luke, leave it."

But Luke had stooped down and was levering the trap open. "Made in Britain," he said in a cold fury. "We're good at this sort of thing." It took all his strength. "I've never seen one as big as this – not to trap animals."

"Barbaric. Is it legal to do that?"

Luke released the dead squirrel from the steel teeth. He shook it away. There was blood on his fingers which he wiped in pine needles. He stood up, eyes fixed on the trap. "It's not legal to set those things for people."

"For people?"

"It's a man-trap. Too big for squirrels or foxes. Step on one of those . . ."

She decided he was trying to scare her. "Man-traps went out with Queen Victoria . . . didn't they?"

It was getting dark. "You want to go on, Pete?"

Petra's answer was to unbutton the case of her Minolta. "Right. Inquiry into Sinister Occurrences in Furmiston Forest: Exhibit Number One." She took a picture of the trap.

As an afterthought, Luke said, "And that thing's just been oiled."

A quarter of a mile further into the forest, the track bent northwards. It progressed for a short distance and then opened into a vast clearing, recently made. There were huge piles of newly-felled trees stacked at the forest edge. Tree stumps had been bulldozed and tons of clinker had been laid to form a wide road surface across the clearing.

"There's another clearing after this one – is that where the mineshafts are?" They crouched in a perfect camouflage of ferns, one pine row in.

"A bit beyond that, I'd guess."

A screen of trees separated the two clearings, leaving

73

a gap wide enough for heavy vehicles. "It's like a military camp." Petra pointed across the clearing towards a complex of wooden buildings. "Workers' huts? Offices?" Adjoining the nearest hut were two diesel oil tanks. "And you knew nothing about all this, Luke Waller!" He did not argue. "You've got to hand it to them, Luke. These people know their business."

"Over there, see? A watch tower going up. Couldn't be a prison?"

"And the trucks are twentieth-century slave-ships? No – it's to do with the mines."

"Everything that counts is through the gap." Luke used his binoculars. "Take a look at the hardware." A massive forest clearance was under way.

Petra brought into focus earthmovers, tractors and pick-up trucks. "Yellow monsters. Like a mechanical zoo." Work had finished for the day. The forest had been driven back, the edges bulldozed, the tree trunks stacked in triangular mountains. "Weird. Everything as still as Sleeping Beauty."

There was no need of binoculars to spot the next discovery. "Floodlights! Second-house has started. Got it – dog-racing!"

Petra was for moving closer.

"There'll be guards."

"We've come this far. No point going back with only a couple of slides of a bulldozer."

They skirted the second clearing, eyes on the ground most of the time, fearful of steel straps Made in Britain. "It seems they're planning to concrete over your wonderful forest, Luke."

"A landing strip?"

In daylight they would have sighted it earlier, but only now, a hundred yards from the circle of floodlight, did they recognise an inner fence.

"It's a crowner!" One ring of concrete posts, armed with steel-mesh and topped with barbed wire, stood a few feet inside the other; and between the fences the ground was laid with barbed wire coils.

Luke felt cold. Through the binoculars he saw double steel gates and beyond them, the biggest mechanical animal of all – a huge mobile crane mounted on steel tracks. "Brontosaurus Rex."

Petra was also focusing on the crane, through her long-throw lens. "No. Tyrannosaurus Rex – Jesus! All this and nobody knows a thing about it."

Cold; and frightened. Enough to start shivering. Have we broken into somebody's nightmare?

"There's something else."

Oh no. Please don't let there be anything else. Luke felt he had made enough exciting discoveries for one night. He let Petra have the binoculars. She was the opposite: this far wasn't far enough.

"Concrete walls. Right in the centre. Like a bunker. Could it be the head of the mineshaft?" She gave him a gentle punch. "Not scared, are you?"

"Aren't you?"

"Course I am. Being scared does you good sometimes. Here, you're the bird-watcher. Take a look."

He focused past the old tips, some of them smothered in coarse grass. He made out a stack of equipment rescued from the mines – lumps of winding gear, iron trucks and rails; and his own memory of his last visit to the minehead, at least five years ago, took his gaze to the central working. "Yes, a concrete bunker . . . They'll have reinforced the shaft, then provided a shield from the weather."

"It's more than a shield. What if it's an underground city? Hey – this could be where the Top Lot will take shelter if the bomb drops."

75

"How are they going to get here if there's a four-minute warning – by British Rail?"

Inside the double fence were two guards, both armed, one escorted by an Alsatian on a leash. Otherwise the camp was deserted.

"They must be eating . . . Check!"

"Check?"

"Twix. I'm in need of glucose." They squatted down on pine sponge earth. "We'll need to get closer when the trucks arrive." She touched his ankle with her foot. "I can feel your heart thudding through the ground. What about mine?"

He stared at her and only smiled. If his heart was thumping, it was partly because of her: I'm falling from a great height. Already he was sensing how time was running away from him; another few days and she would be out of his life. In future, everything would be BP and AP – Before Pete and After Pete. Treasure the moment. And all this disturbed his calm: was it treasuring the moment, or risking it?

She lay on her side, eyes watchful for any movement in the camp. "We've a play about mineshafts. The Siren Sisters did it when we were in Cornwall. Mineshafts and – blood. There's this giant called Bolster. He's had a thousand wives. Takes a new one every year after stoning the last one to death on St Agnes' Beacon – that's in Cornwall.

"As it was my birthday, they let me play Jecholiah, his thousandth wife who decides she doesn't want a chunk of granite in the head. So she has a quiet word with St Agnes, because Aggy rather objects to so many female deaths on her beacon . . . Now Bolster likes to relax by blood-letting, taking a razor to his vein and leaning his arm over one of the old leadmine shafts. Then, refreshed, he gets up and does in his poor wifey.

"Not on this occasion, though. Jecholiah charms our

giant, feeds him with a mammoth breakfast – cow pie, actually, which Ron made for our Desperate Dan sketch – and persuades him to tap off a little of his blood into this very special mineshaft. She puts his great head into her lap and sings to him so sweetly he falls fast asleep – like you'll do unless I finish this story quick.

"Nearby is the ocean and Jecholiah knows her trick is working when the sea begins to be dyed red – for the blood now fills the shaft; it pours through underground passages until the sea is deep scarlet, and Bolster is weaker than a kitten . . . He tries to struggle, stands as high as the Frost Demon, but his life force is gone. He crashes to the ground and makes it shudder for a hundred miles around. How about that?"

"What happened to Jecholiah – did she become Prime Minister?"

Absolute stillness, disturbed only by the pines shifting against one another in the night wind off the moors. Then, three short whistle blasts. Petra and Luke leapt up. They dodged further into the forest, steel traps forgotten.

"The circus is arriving in town. Let's get along there and give them a wave." Indeed the circle of floodlights within the double fence resembled a circus ring. At the centre of it was a sole performer, the giant crane, now being approached by more workmen. These were clad differently from their colleagues arriving from the billets. "Like astronauts," said Petra. They wore red boiler suits and black masks.

Through the binoculars Luke spotted a notice on the outer fence beside the swing gates. He read it out:

EXTREME DANGER
AUTHORISED PERSONNEL ONLY

The guards were unlocking the inner gate, pegging back. The crane was on the move, away from its parking position close to the concrete bunker and towards levelled ground to the side of the gates, halting, adjusting direction, progressing; watched by the strange figures in red and black.

"See those logs? We'll get a great view." Petra tapped her third-hand Minolta. "And great pictures."

"They could see us crossing."

"Fifteen yards from cover, that's all."

More like twenty-five, but he didn't argue. She was determined, and moving down the defile of firs. From the Wynster end of the forest came the sound of trucks.

"What?" Luke thought she was joking.

"Go on, or do you want me to do it for you?" She had dug for damp earth beneath the dry, smeared her face with it. She rubbed what remained against Luke's cheeks and daubed his forehead, finishing the job with a tweak of his nose. "You look very pretty."

As the sound of the siren faded, the trucks appeared on perfect cue: two tall-sided container lorries escorted by the Toyota Landcruiser. "Now!" Petra grabbed Luke's arm. "Don't fall in nettles again." She sprinted, with Luke slow-tailing behind, but still there and nettle-free. She turned, gathered him in, spared him a hug of excitement and relief. "Better than watching telly any day, eh?"

"I wouldn't know. They took ours back." He leaned along the slope of the logs, burying his mouth in his sleeve. I'm a very scared person.

"Still got the pine cone?" He nodded. "Then we'll be okay." Her long-throw lens was poised. "As soon as they come into the light . . ."

Once the trucks had reached the outer clearing, the Landcruiser pulled off to the right, in the direction of the billets and the office. A foreman in yellow overalls and helmet waited at the junction between two clearings. He signalled the trucks through.

The gates of the inner and outer fence were wide open. The guards were outside, facing the track. The trucks slowly advanced. The foreman, carrying a clipboard, followed them along until the first truck stopped thirty yards from the gates.

All the while, Petra was taking pictures. "These'll look terrific on Ron's superscreen." She smiled. "I got a nice one of Don's profile. He's really rather attractive."

The driver of the first truck had got down. He was being replaced by one of the men inside the fence. Meanwhile, Don had entered the camp office. He switched on an electric light. "All mod cons," said Luke watching through the binoculars.

"We'll have to poke around in that office, Luke. If we've a chance."

I just think I want to go home.

"What?"

"I didn't say anything."

"Yes you did – to yourself. You said we're pushing our luck."

Truck number one was passing through the double fence; and the giant crane was tracking forward to meet it. On either side advanced the workmen in red and black. Two of them carried steel scaling ladders which they fixed in place against the container. The men climbed the ladders and met on the roof.

"They're unzipping it!"

The shell of tough black PVC was not so much unzipped as untied, and the top of this gigantic parcel unrolled to reveal a metallic casing beneath. Aluminium, thought Luke.

The crane approached as noisily as a tank squadron. Its

hook glinted in the lights. "Damn, I've reached twenty-four." Petra turned her back on the scene, leaned against the logs and rewound her film. "Tell me what's happening."

"Looks like a game of Chinese Boxes – one container inside another. There goes the aluminium box. They're folding the sides underneath. Very neat. Don't rush – you've time."

"Right." Petra's camera was soon back in action. "Chinese Boxes, I like that. Or Russian dolls. So what charming little princess is inside?"

A second set of walls was being removed. Workmen on all sides were using hydraulic tools to unstopper bolted seams. "Oh hell."

"Vicars' sons don't use that word. What's up?"

"That sign." He handed the binoculars to her, but her eye was glued to the camera. "You know what it means, Pete?"

She did. "I can't believe it. She shook her head. "No. We've got to be mistaken."

From the base of the container at the heart of the Chinese Boxes, the workmen in their black protective masks had uncoiled chains which had been traced up through reinforced steel hoops.

"So that's what they look like – a central heating system . . . Or rather a central cooling system. Horrible." She turned to Luke. "You know what I'm thinking?"

He nodded. "That we're in deep."

"Which means these pictures are – "

"You'll never be able to use them."

"What? After all the trouble we've taken?"

The crane hook had been lowered to a position three feet above the container and the chains fed on to the hook. The workmen returned to ground. The crane took the strain, slowly, slowly; and the container rose, gleaming, panelled with cooling pipes, angling gently.

"So it's not Giant Bolster's blood they're burying." She paused in her picture-taking, shocked by the enormity of their discovery. "Now we can understand their secrecy." She shivered. "They'd kill us, Luke, if they knew we'd found out."

The crane was carrying the nuclear waste to its burial ground.

On Petra's lips, as she and Luke returned from the circus lights, were the words, "Nobody'll believe us. The pictures will help, but we need more information." Who owned the forest? Where was the waste coming from? Who organised its passage? What kind of nuclear waste was it? And how dangerous?

Was this dumping legal?

They agreed, it was wise to get back to Wynster; take no more chances. But then they saw Don Neeson leaving the camp office. With Paddy, he got in the Landcruiser and headed along the pine avenue towards the outer fence.

"It's our chance, Luke."

"And crazy."

She had suggested they make for the office. It was empty. The clearing was deserted. "We need names. Maybe there'll be despatch sheets . . . I'll photograph them."

"With the light on?"

"No, with the flash."

"And bring people running? You're off your head."

"Look, we can never come back. So we must make the best of it. Unless we can name names, we'll get shown the door."

Luke surprised himself. "Make it quick, then."

They passed from the second to the first clearing. They were in darkness now. They watched, waited, then glided into the open. A wooden walkway had been laid along the front of the barrack huts. The office was the end one, siding on to the forest. Here there was the start of a further clearing.

As Petra and Luke approached, they could make out the beginnings of what looked like an assault course – a wall of planks, a deep-cut ditch with a wooden frame over it and ropes hanging in line. Beyond was a rope scaling net. "To keep the macho boys fit," whispered Petra. "And stop them getting bored."

They circled the office, coming up to it from the rear. Petra had hoped there might be a back window. No luck. "It's got to be in through the front."

Luke found himself hoping the office door would be tightly locked. They could then retire with honour; and in one piece. No luck. There was not even a tell-tale squeak as Petra unlatched the door and edged it open. "Keep an eye."

Only one eye? Not *Pygmalion* likely. Both eyes, wide as they would go, X-raying the dark. He could hear Petra's feet; a shuffling sound; the slur of a metal drawer. Be quick. He suddenly wanted a piss. He felt the flash of the Minolta as much as he saw it. Not too many of those, please.

And then he saw the guard. "Pete!" Luke tried to muzzle his voice with one hand, directing the sound from his palm. The guard was armed, strolling from the next clearing. He was smoking, in no hurry. "Pete . . . Don't!" Got to go inside. He turned, pressed the latch.

Petra had hesitated at the sight of him. "I've an address – London."

He whispered; "Please don't take any more." He pointed over his shoulder with clenched fist and thumb. The door was ajar. Luke closed it. We're trapped.

"See him?"

Luke stayed beside the window. One eye peered out: nothing. That was worse, for he knew the guard was closer.

"Should we run?"

He shook his head. There was a lot of forest outside, miles of brambles in blind dark. Anyway, it was too late. There were footfalls on the walkway. Between the filing cabinet and the wall there was a space. They moved into it instinctively; crouched, turned faces to the wall.

The office door was opened, halfway then fully. The light was switched on. Petra remembered she had not closed the desk drawer. She could see nothing but dark green metal, a loose stud, a splash of correction fluid. Luke could see nothing but the tangle of Petra's hair and her one silver earring.

Two heavy paces: the guard approached the desk. There was a pause, a listening, then the desk drawer was shut rapidly. "Not like you, Mr Neeson." Two more steps: no chance, for this would bring the guard in a line with the trespassers. Petra dared to look up, ready to flinch, to shut her eyes at the moment of discovery.

Yet the footsteps had been back to the door. Again, there was a pause; a last look round; a smell of tobacco; a creaking floorboard – and then the light-switch returned the room to darkness.

They listened to the footsteps receding along the walkway. They breathed out, collapsing into each other. "Remind me ..." She had no breath and scarcely enough strength to straighten her legs. "Not to do this too often."

Compared to the hot-spot Luke and Petra had survived during the last few minutes, the return journey to the outer fence was to be an excursion. After two hundred yards they took to the track. "We made it!" Luke shared with Petra a wild sense of relief, and of achievement. "We came through fire, Luke."

He chose his words more cautiously, "We got lucky

. . . It's a great feeling." Even better, he thought, than risking a rockface and reaching the top.

"Now you know why people like danger."

"Or why some knock their heads against brick walls – it's wonderful when you stop."

"What I'm glad about, Luke, is that we went through it together."

Yes, he appreciated that too: it would be the memory of this night he would cherish the most.

They slipped in among the trees a quarter of a mile from the gate. "Funny. When you're excited, you can see better in the dark."

"Certainly beats carrots."

They had no difficulty locating the pine brand that marked their passage to freedom. "Easy." They traced the Navigator under its blanket of ferns.

"Check," said Luke.

"Check?"

He touched her cheek and his own. "Two heads still in place." They wheeled the motorcycle through the firs, each step, each wheel-turn taking them from the fence, calming nerves, slowing pulses. They smelt the drift of pine. They heard the crack of the wind far above them.

They were exultant still, but kept their celebration silent as they mounted the Navigator and free-wheeled down towards the track. "The trucks won't be out for ages."

Before kicking her machine into action, and deafening the wind, Petra said, "Thanks for the company, partner."

Luke put his arms round her waist. He stared ahead of him at the empty track. "Take it easy, eh?"

"I'll do my best. Nortons aren't fieldmice." She accelerated away. Luke closed his eyes. Almost fieldmouse, he thought. Down the straightening track. Easy.

The mud ruts deepened where a wide firebreak cut

northwards through the forest. Petra slowed, manoeuvred carefully – and had her eyes on the ground at the instant that a single glance up the firebreak would have revealed the presence of the Landcruiser, patiently and darkly waiting among the firs.

The motorcycle, its rider and its passenger, sped on.

Don Neeson's view of the Unapproachable Norton was brief but uninterrupted. It was Paddy who spoke:

"That's a fiver I owe you, Don . . ."

These days, the Reverend Alfred Waller never went to bed before two or three in the morning. Even if he did, he could not sleep. He brooded on Vera, on her absence. "It's the witching hour," he would say, "When my darker thoughts entertain one another." Now he brooded on his son, and Petra, the intruder in their lives. "A mixed blessing," Alfred had concluded. Vera doesn't come, so she wishes this creature on us. Beautiful. Captivating, but strangely dangerous. A sort of Pied Piper in skirts, except that she doesn't actually wear skirts, luring us – Luke in particular – to . . . I'm not sure what . . . Heaven or Hell.

There was a knock on the door. A caller, at one o'clock, and coming to the front door? Only the police or hikers seeking a bed for the night ever called at the front door. The knock was repeated. "Coming." If it's old Hartfield again, complaining about Vera booking a bunch of jailbirds for the Carnival, I'll dunk him in his own elderflower wine. Horrible stuff. "Yes?"

Don Neeson stood a pace back from the open door. It had stuck as usual, then shuddered against Alfred's toe. He bit back the cry of pain. "Reverend Waller?"

"That's right."

"My name's Neeson – I'm sorry to disturb you so late, but it is a matter of some considerable urgency."

"Concerning?"

"Your son – and his young lady."

"I see. Would you care to step in?" Alfred noticed, beyond the garden wall, another man, hovering, but with no intention of coming any closer.

"For a few moments, yes."

Alfred's instinct was not to trust this young man; and he sensed the tension beneath a veneer of politeness and deference. They entered the poorly-lit kitchen. On the table were photo albums which Alfred had been flicking through, dwelling on happier times. "I'm sorry." He cleared the albums away. "Please sit down, Mr . . . er?"

"Neeson." Don sat at the corner of the table, under the light. His blond hair was dark at the roots. His cord blouson gleamed a deep emerald. "I'll come directly to the point, Reverend. I'm head of Security at the Furmiston Project, and I've evidence that the two of them broke through the perimeter fence this evening. That is a criminal offence and we are considering bringing a charge against them, of causing material damage and entering private property."

To protect his son, Alfred lied: "Luke would never do a thing like that."

"On his own, perhaps not – but influenced by the redhead, maybe?"

Alfred's confidence was on the slide. "What . . . evidence are you referring to?"

"They were seen leaving Furmiston at precisely ten thirty-five. We inspected the perimeter fence and found over three foot of it cut – a pricey matter to put right."

"But you didn't actually see them cut the fence?"

"Security staff man the gates, Mr Waller. They constitute witnesses."

"I see. You mean they'd be willing to swear in a court of law that they saw my son snip the wire?"

Don Neeson waited; fought with his natural impatience.

He got up from his chair. He seemed unusually tall in this poor light. "If necessary . . . it occurs to me, it would not look good in the papers – a *family* of wire-snippers."

"What do you mean?"

"Your wife's in the same business, I believe."

Alfred was numb. "Who are you?"

"Someone who wishes to go quietly about his legitimate business, Reverend. Whose company has no more desire to drag silly kids through the courts than I imagine you want to see the lad in dock."

"Is that the only reason? And who, pray, is this company that's fencing off half the countryside?"

On these questions, Don remained silent. His stern eye defied further argument; and Alfred felt bad, incapable of pressing his case, for he had lied: he knew of Luke's escapade with Petra. They'd been full of it, told him every detail; stirred alarm in him and the first traces of anger. Yet his alarm and anger were little in comparison with the fear – indeed terror – aroused by the prospect of Luke getting into trouble with the police.

"Do we have your word, Reverend?"

"My word?" He was getting as bad as Luke for repeating other people's questions.

"We shall not press charges if we can be assured – "

"I'll talk to them." He was brisk now; as angry at Luke and Petra for landing him in this embarrassment as suspicious of this man who looked and talked and behaved like either a hit-man or a soldier of fortune. "There'll be no more trouble, rest assured."

"And the young lady?"

"She is a guest in my house." He risked a joke. "I shall inform her it's no longer a haven for terrorists, however young and pretty."

The word did not go down well with Don. Perhaps he was congenitally incapable of smiling. "Be sure," he said;

and the tone of his voice was clear – be sure or else. He headed down the passage to the front door. There was a last item on his agenda. He turned at the open door. Paddy stood waiting beside the Landcruiser. "According to the posters all over town, Reverend, you're holding a carnival."

Relieved to come off the defensive at last, Alfred failed to see the trip-wire at his feet. "Oh yes . . . Been planning it for months. A *Grand* Carnival, actually. A day of fun for all the family. To cheer up the town, take their minds off some of the dreadful things happening at home and abroad."

"Very salutary, Reverend. Our company will no doubt make a generous contribution to any charities you're collecting for."

"Africa, mainly."

"Yes, Africa."

"Not to mention the school roof . . ."

And now the trip-wire.

"But a word of warning to the banner wavers and whatever protest groups turn up – steer them clear of Furmiston. They'll not be welcome."

Alfred laughed, yet not convincingly. "I'm the vicar round here, not the SAS."

Don Neeson was as unamused as ever. "But you read me?"

Alfred felt chilled to the heart. He watched the man go. There had been no handshake. Yes, Alfred read him. He understood. His words dropped feebly into silence:

"Thanks for calling."

Chapter 5

Petra had expected the university would be deserted, yet it was as busy as in term-time, full of summer courses and conferences. It had been a lucky break: until Petra's sister had had baby Michael, she worked as secretary to the head of the university's science faculty. "Professor Schutzman?"

"Ah, Pete, is it? I was told to look out for a head on fire."

"It's very kind of you to see me."

"I've a selfish motive. I need Lena back in the office to sort out the chaos." Professor Schutzman glanced at his watch. He had just come from addressing a conference of American science students. "I can spare you half an hour, Pete, then I must skid off to the airport. Oslo next stop. You want a coffee?"

Petra had left Wynster Bridge that morning at six. Luke had persuaded Jim Crabtree, lorry driver at Monarch, to add Petra to his load of Satin Finish on the London run. She had phoned Lena during a tea-stop at Watford Gap. "I'm on to a story that'll win me a Pulitzer Price for ace reporting. Can you put me up for a night or two – and what's your dishy professor called?"

As Professor Schutzman prepared coffee in his study overlooking a leafy quadrangle, Petra mused, I always thought academics were musty old sticks with beards and a stammer, and who kept knocking things over. This one's not only got his heart in the right place, according to Lena, but he's a nice face and a gorgeous bum: who said beauty and brains don't mix?

"So you're doing a project, Pete, on the Chernobyl

disaster? The world's worst accident. I thought people had forgotten all about it."

"Well, not Chernobyl exactly ... It's a bit closer to home. Not so much nuclear explosions as ... nuclear waste." She explained about the camp in Furmiston Forest, about the barbed wire fence, the trucks, the guards and the floodlights; and she described what took place inside the inner fence, the use of the giant crane to lift and lower the weird pipe-clad metal container.

The rush of her words faltered. "It's not all bullshit, Professor – honestly!"

"Okay, show me on the map where all this is happening ... Ah, limestone country."

"There's an old leadmine. Shafts running in all directions. I mean, is it possible?"

"Strictly illegal. Definitely not advisable – but possible, especially considering public hostility to officially designated dumping sites."

"Is it dangerous?"

"Put it this way – how dangerous is an unexploded bomb? Nuclear waste may be deemed safe until it leaks, then it becomes potentially the most harmful substance on earth. So the question is, can you make sure it doesn't leak, or isn't disturbed? Of course much depends on the level of toxicity – high level, intermediate or low level."

"So this could just be low-level waste – not very dangerous?"

"In the smallest quantities, radioactive substances are dangerous, if they aren't properly and securely stored."

"What kind of things would low-level waste be?"

"Typically, contaminated machine parts, aprons, tissues, gloves, paper – and getting rid of the stuff is a major headache, growing every day."

Petra's black notebook was open. "How major?"

"By AD 2000, it's been estimated, there'll be over a

billion cubic feet of such wastes queuing up for disposal – enough, American analysts have calculated, to cover a four-lane highway from coast to coast in the States to a depth of four feet."

The professor warmed to his subject. "If it's liquid waste, it's kept on site in the power stations in tanks like swimming pools. Low-level can be dumped in trenches or kept in steel drums – and that's the problem: the containers are subject to corrosion."

"You mean they leak – but after how long?"

Professor Schutzmann poured out coffee. "You'll not find a scientist who'd trust any material beyond fifteen or twenty years." He smiled. "When this question crops up, I always think of the pyramids – built to last for ever, and to keep out the tomb robbers. Some hope! In my view, it doesn't matter what you store nuclear waste in – glass, ceramic, aluminium, you name it – there are too many unpredictables.

"If you lock the stuff underground in reinforced concrete, you still face the hazards of time – earth movement, underground streams; and what happens if, over the centuries, people forget that the waste deposits are there? If, for example, new geological drilling takes place?"

"But why centuries?"

"Because that's how long some materials take to lose their radioactive power. Take the decay chain of uranium – 234, for instance. You'd have to wait a quarter of a million years before it was safe."

"Is that the worst?"

"Idione–129 would need a million years – almost back to the dinosaurs."

"Tyrannosarus Rex?"

"Absolutely."

Petra sat upright, stilled by these words. The information was spreading through her head. "Then a place like Furmiston Forest, even if it's low-level waste . . ." The idea dawned. "The dump would have to be under strict security for hundreds of years?"

The professor nodded. He watched Petra's face. It was registering the full enormity of the problem. "If the Romans had buried nuclear waste, we'd still be guarding it."

She was thinking, what if there were to be lots of Furmistons? She asked:

"Just what happens if – you touch it, touch the stuff?"

"Or inhale it . . . Initial symptons – nausea, vomiting, intense headache, dizziness. Acute flu, only worse. Of course it's all dose-dependent. Those trapped within the immediate vicinity of the Chernobyl Number 4 reactor when it exploded were doomed to die within hours. But serious leaks are not uncommon at all nuclear power stations. Sellafield in Cumbria, for instance – has an appalling record.

"Acute radiation exposure from dosages in the region of a thousand to three thousand rems leads to the so-called 'gastro-intestinal syndrome': in two weeks you're dead from circulatory collapse. More than three thousand rems, and you're dead in forty-eight hours. Your hair will probably have fallen out, your skin haemorrhaged, your bladder ceased to be waterproof."

The professor paused, drank, continued. "The real question mark hangs over the effects of long-term dosage: cancers – leukaemia especially; genetic defects, birth abnormalities."

Petra stopped writing. She wanted to duck for cover.

"There's no such thing as a safe level, you see. Experiments on dogs in 1974, where three millionths of a gram of plutonium–238 was embedded in their tissues, induced lung cancer."

"Still," tried Petra, "if people are kept well away,

92

and the waste is locked in steel and earth and watched over –?"

"Well, you tell me . . . What happens in your leadmine with its maze of tunnels if an underground stream happens to wash over steel drums, maybe because of unusually heavy rains? You've heard of brine?"

"Salt?"

"Salt water – it's a steel-eater, there's nothing more corrosive. Sooner or later, then, the drums leak. And the underground stream passes on its way, joining surface streams, which feed into reservoirs and rivers; which irrigate the land.

"Are you with me, Pete? Grass grows, cows eat it. Cows produce milk which humans drink – strontium-90. Being chemically like calcium, strontium will seek out and become incorporated in bone, and for the unfortunate ones the result is leukaemia."

For another five minutes Professor Schutzman added detail to disconcerting detail, then he pushed back his chair. Time was up. "I want you to keep in touch, Pete. As things stand, I doubt very much whether any private company would take the risk of establishing a nuclear dump without official approval. It could simply be toxic chemicals, though I must say I'm amazed that they're taking the precautions you've described."

The professor's suitcase stood by his desk. He offered Petra a firm and friendly handshake, and they went out together into the heat and dust and noise of the city. "Pete," he cautioned at the parting of the ways, "don't dream of taking on this thing alone. The nuclear business involves millions of pounds. It's tough and as pressures grow to dispose of waste, it'll get increasingly ruthless.

"When I get back from Oslo, I'll start a few inquiries of my own. In the meantime, don't play Tom Thumb among the giants."

She watched him go down a mineshaft of another sort, into the gloomy shades of the Underground. She shrugged. "I'm only writing a play about it."

"Dad? I'm being followed."

Alfred looked up from Vera's letter which gave a cheerful account of her prison visit to the Sisters. 'Wait till they hit Wynster,' she had written. 'They'll really stir up the sediment.' This had cast Alfred into a depression. Wasn't one of the Siren Sisters enough? Petra alone was proving more than the old town could cope with.

Sediment? We're already choking on it.

"Not by that Don character?"

"No. A sandy-haired bloke in a green Escort. He's everywhere. He was outside Monarch at lunchtime. He followed me up to Connie's after work."

"But it's Don's man, yes? Then my word's not good enough."

"They're just making sure. Put the frights on me a bit. I'm not bothered . . . as long as they don't tamper with Pete's machine."

Luke was thoughtful for a moment. "They must be wondering where Pete is." He was suddenly uneasy. If they're tailing me, that's fine, I'm not up to much; which makes Pete the target.

Alfred seemed to have read his son's thoughts. "She's pulling the tail of the tiger, Luke."

"Warned you?"

"Kind of."

"I should think so." Lena said. "If there's something illegal going on, Pete, tell the police." She stared at her younger sister. They were bathing the baby together, Petra holding the child up on wonky legs, Lena wiping him gently with a sponge. "Of course you'll do nothing of the sort, will you?"

94

"After what the cops did to me and the Sisters, do you blame me?"

Lena wiped and squeezed, then reached for a towel. "You seem to be pretty smitten by this Luke – what's he like?"

"Quiet."

This earned a laugh. "I thought quiet men bored the pants off you."

"And he's a nature-lover."

"You hate the countryside!"

"Not any longer. He's a way of changing your mind. People think he's a dreamer, but underneath he's nobody's pushover."

"Talking of nobody – nobody has a vicar for a dad these days."

"That's what I told him. He said he'd tried to trade Alfred in for a war hero, but there were no volunteers."

"Quick?"

"Some of the time, but not when his mother Vera's around. Then he acts like a prime candidate for a remedial class."

Lena gazed at her own child. She addressed him proudly: "I wonder what brave cause would make me desert you, my pet?" She wrapped the baby and put it into Petra's arms. "Or am I being unfair?"

"A little. Luke can look after himself."

"And Luke's dad?"

"He's having more difficulty. But he's trying hard." Petra followed Lena's gaze which had rested on a framed photograph on the chest of drawers: their own father.

"I miss him, Pete. All the time."

Petra kissed her sister. "Me, too ... But he's there when we want him."

"You really believe that, don't you?"

"He said he would: Dad never lied to us."

Their hands touched. "Believe it, pet," Lena said.

"Mr Rhodes? There's a young woman asking to see you. She says she's a newspaper reporter."

"Press? What on earth could she want?"

"She refuses to say exactly, sir, but claims it's a matter of considerable urgency."

"Tell her if she won't divulge her interest, I won't see her."

There was a pause before the secretary returned with more information. "She says it is about the Furmiston Forest Project in Wynster Bridge."

"Ask her to come back next week."

"She says she's only in London till Friday, Mr Rhodes."

"Take her name, then, and the newspaper she represents . . . Oh, Miss Searle, what does this woman look like – is she a redhead?"

"Yes sir, very much so."

"Then keep her waiting . . . Say I might be able to see her in – thirty minutes. Delay her another ten minutes and then boot her out. Explain that pressing business prevents me seeing her till next month."

The Managing Director (UK) of Disposal Services International now made a long-distance call. "Mr Cassidy, please. Thank you . . . Charles Rhodes, London-end here, sir. How are you? Fine, fine, except for the heat. They're even predicting an earthquake or two . . ! It's the WB Forest Project – a trifling piece of trouble, but worth mentioning, perhaps. We had a break-in a couple of nights ago. Nothing serious – two teenage kamikazi. We've put in half a dozen more heavy personnel. And we're debating whether to create a dry moat of barbed wire along the inside of the perimeter fence."

"Not a trifle, then, Charlie?"

"Till this morning, we were pretty confident the matter

was settled. However, my secretary tells me that we have one of the young gangsters downstairs at this minute, posing as a journalist."

"Sounds too enterprising for a British teenager."

"This one's a politico. Belongs to a theatrical group that gets steamed up over environmental issues."

"They can all be bought off with something or other, Charlie. Anyhow, you know the procedure."

"They've received a first warning, sir."

"Okay, then operate the safety mechanism."

Colonel Richard Prynge Tattershall, Member of Parliament for Rowmanton and Wynster, was called from the Members' Bar of the House of Commons to receive a petition brought by one of his constituents. He was intrigued: the people of Row and Steer, as he affectionately referred to his long-held parliamentary seat, occasionally wrote letters of complaint about potholes in roads or poor street lighting, but this was the very first time he had been presented with a petition.

He was greeted by a rather fetching young woman with brilliant copper hair, wearing her sister's skirt and high heels, and a pair of blue-framed spectacles. She was holding a sheaf of A4 paper.

"Only one of us was permitted to see you, Sir Richard."

Colonel Tattershall accepted this sudden elevation to a knighthood as being only his due (indeed, considering his years of service to the Party and the Nation, it was overdue): "A petition from Rowmanton and Wynster? My goodness, what is it about, young lady?"

"Dumping."

"Dumping?"

"Yes – dumping toxic wastes in Furmiston Forest."

Tattershall reached out for the papers. "That's a surprise. Furmiston, eh?"

Petra kept tight hold of her papers on which she had got the genuine signatures of not more than twenty-five people so far. The sheets fattening the pile were blanks. "Furmiston Forest actually runs alongside property owned by your family, I believe, Mr Tattershall."

This abrupt demotion from Sir to Mister was of less concern to Colonel Tattershall than the provocative tone of the young woman's question. "How many names, er, Miss?"

"Scales . . . Well, we're hoping to get the signatures of every voter in Wynster Bridge."

" 'We'? And who's 'we' when we're at home? Friends of the Earth? Greenpeace?"

Petra didn't want to get either of these organisations into trouble just yet. "Friends of Furmiston," she said. She slipped the petition neatly back into Lena's leather briefcase. "This was simply to let you know what we are doing, and to inform you that the whole town is getting truly, er, burned up and browned off about the goings-on in Furmiston."

"Young lady – you surprise me utterly. What are people alleging is being dumped at Furmiston? And if the place is private property and properly secured, what business is it of the citizens of Wynster Bridge or anywhere else?"

"That's what we'd like you to look into, Major."

This time he did object: "Colonel, if you please."

"The company is Disposal Services International." Petra was retreating slowly. A minute more of this and she would be unmasked. "Which belongs to an even bigger multi-national, Star Oil."

Colonel Tattershall was impatient to be gone. "Miss Scales, you appear to forget that I belong to a party which is in *favour* of private enterprise. And of letting people get on with the job. Now, if you'll excuse me –"

"Even if the enterprise is nuclear waste?"

"Friends of the Earth. Good afternoon?"

"I'm a reporter and I'd like to talk to someone about whether it's legal to dump nuclear waste in old leadmines."

"Greenpeace?"

"Speaking."

"I'm writing a TV script on what would happen if nuclear waste, stored in tunnels under a small town, began to leak."

"*Guardian* Science Editor speaking . . ."

"*New Statesman*, Reporters . . ."

"*New York Times*, London office . . ."

"BBC . . ."

"ITN Newsdesk – who's speaking, please?"

"Mr Rhodes? There's a caller on the line from Friends of the Earth . . ."

"Mr Rhodes? It's Greenpeace. Same message as before, is it?"

"Absolutely. In fact, block all further calls today."

"Mr Rhodes?"

"What is it this time? I really don't want – "

"Colonel Tattershall, sir, MP for Rowmanton and Wynster."

"Put him through . . . Richard?"

"Charles, I've had the BBC on to me – what the hell's going on?"

"Pete? It's Luke."

"At last! I thought you'd forgotten about me. Have you missed me?"

"It's been quiet."

"You know what I mean."

"The answer's yes. Dad's hovering. We've not paid the last phone bill. All I want to say is, without trying to put the wind up you – I'm being followed. So you might be too."

"Hadn't noticed, but what do you advise – for me to scatter rabbit droppings?" She said she planned to return north Friday evening. "I've promised to babysit for Lena and Sam tonight. Tomorrow I'll draft out my play script."

"I'll fetch you from the station, and I'll stay by the phone once you've left London."

Lena, full of last-minute instructions before going out with Sam to dinner: "If Michael wakes, Pete, he'll insist on a feed and then a jog on your knee for twenty minutes. Put him straight down, leave the bedside light on."

"Shove off, both of you, I'll manage."

"We won't be late."

"Be as late as you like. You're looking a dream, Sam."

Lena thought so too. "Here, phone number of the restaurant – Billy the Greek's. Don't hesitate to ring – "

"Stop fussing." Through a parted curtain, Petra and her nephew waved as Lena and Sam rocked away in their exhaust-coughing Toledo. They watched it halt at the street end and screech into a blaze of London traffic.

The curtain did not fall entirely back into place. The sliver of light it left was noted with satisfaction by the occupants of an unlit Sierra parked below and opposite.

The phone rang a few minutes later. "Sam and Lena Ngitewa's residence." Petra got no answering voice. "Hello?" She waited, then replaced the phone, staring at it. Now she noticed the gap in the curtain. She closed it. Michael was silent in his cot. Petra turned off the light. She returned to the window, opened the curtain and glanced down.

In her thoughts, Luke's words. Considerate of him not to put the wind up me. Now you mention it, Luke . . . She saw a man emerge from the phone-box at the end of the street. He approached on the near side of the road, then crossed to the Sierra.

Thanks, Mr Rhodes, so now I know the worst.

With a fair wind rising, Petra darted through the flat to

100

check the outer door. The catch was down. She fitted the chain. Admit it, you're shaking.

It's having the baby here. And in apartments like this – whoever hears you scream for help?

She noticed a rubber door wedge. There was fire in her mind, bottles of it, or burning paper soaked in petrol. She stuffed the wedge hard into the letterbox. One action sparked another. She heaved the hallstand in front of the door and supported this with a black wooden bedding box.

Thank God we're on the second floor.

Yet she suddenly burst through into the kitchen whose outer door opened on to a fire escape. It was all glass and easy handles, and the stairs emptied into a dank backyard full of dustbins.

This is all I need.

She removed the kitchen door key, dragged a cupboard against the door, piled it with every obstacle she could lay her hands on.

She twisted round in terror as the front doorbell rang. She froze, waited, stared. The doorbell rang again, insolently long. They were trying the letterbox, thrusting at it, striking at the steel flap. But the rubber wedge held. All Petra could hear was the steam pump of her heart, near rupture.

Again the door bell ran, on and on, piercing, till Petra wanted to scream for the first time in her life. A folded paper was pressed under the door. She waited. And waited. Her brain flashed with images of the forest, the Frost Demon, the men in black masks. And she felt as the forest might have done had it a mind of its own – raided, polluted, without the strength to resist.

The ringing had stopped. She ran to the window. She opened the curtain a fraction: two men entering the Sierra. She waited – and the Sierra moved off. She returned to the front door, picked up the note and unfolded it. All it said was:

SEE YOU TOMORROW

It looked as though Luke's tail had been called off. He had come out of Monarch Paints at five-thirty – no green Escort; he had driven over to Rowmanton library – no green Escort; and now he sat beside Boldventure Lake, bathed in red twilight – and still no green Escort.

"I think I'm missing you, Sandy." Yes, about a millionth as much as I'm missing Pete.

This is ridiculous. Two days – and I'm lonely. Never felt like that before. "You're right, Pete, the only child doesn't get lonely." Until he falls in love, that is.

Here's the most stupendous sunset in history, completely wasted without you, Pete. He surveyed the scarlet waters. Our spot, Dad; next to the Frost Demon, our favourite: to watch the water birds, record the rare ones.

Luke reviewed his last conversation with Alfred. "Drop the whole thing, Dad – is that advice or an order?"

"You and Petra are like tadpoles in a pool of carp, Luke. Leave Furmiston to the grown-ups, to the authorities."

"Authorities! They probably know all bout the dumping. Who knows whether they've taken bribes to keep quiet?"

"That's not you talking, Luke. It's Petra. Listen, I want you to speak to her when she gets back. What matters is that the Carnival is a success, not a bloodbath."

Luke had been half-persuaded. On his own, without Pete there to stoke up his mind, things became blurred. What he had read about radiation at the Rowmanton library frightened him. Phrases bounced around in his head: nuclear power stations were, in some writers' views, mere 'bomb factories'; even if they weren't constructed at vast

102

expense to manufacture plutonium for bombs, they were so dangerous, they were 'accidents waiting to happen'.

"Leave well alone." Dad's phrase carried more weight with Luke the more he thought about it. And yet . . .

He dropped down the steep white shore to the water's edge. The question is, do carp eat tadpoles? He stared at the lake. Giant Bolster's blood. He turned to look up the valley. He could not get Bolster out of his mind.

In the story, he recalled, the giant's blood had gushed down the mineshafts. It had poured into underground streams which fed into rivers. Luke examined the landscape as if he had never properly perceived it before. These streams, feeding the lake – they either pass through Furmiston or beneath it.

From Boldventure, the overflow drops into rhododendron woods. Then it becomes Rocky Brook which passes into Sunnyhurst, where there's a paddling pool. Another branch joins the Wynster.

If the waste at Furmiston somehow got into the water . . . Bloodbath, Dad? I'm not sure that's the problem. At least blood is something you can see. He returned to the Navigator – and saw, under the spread of an oak on a farm track, the green Escort.

Okay, Dad, carp do eat tadpoles.

Alfred had never been a fretful parent, worrying all the time where his son had got to. Now, in altered circumstances, he had hung about the garden, getting increasingly restive as evening drifted across the fell.

"Message," he said with ill-disguised relief, when Luke turned up on Pete's machine. "Somebody called Ron, with the Siren Sisters' barge. He'd appreciate a helping hand if you could meet him at Lower Chapel Lock."

"Then will you wait by the phone, Dad – in case Pete calls?"

Alfred nodded. It was a characteristic Luke prized in his father: when asked a favour, he never queried it, and he always did it. "Don't be too long. I've a few calls to make around the parish later on."

"Shake your timbers, landlubber," called Ron. "Stick this one-eyed jackeroo on the torquemada nut and open the gates of Jericho." He slung a lever on to the canal towpath. "Clockwise, Samson!"

"I wasn't born yesterday, Methuselah." Luke walked on to the timber rig of the lock gate. The high water reflected a profile of alders in vermilion and turquoise; the low water was black ink.

To suit the part, Ron was wearing a sea captain's peaked cap as he stood at the wheel of *The Lucky Dragon*. There was a lighted paraffin lamp on the prow, palely competing with the twilight. Its watery echo was a smudge of yellow lapped with woodpecker green and water rat brown.

Luke paused for breath.

"You're out of condition, young Joshua. It must be our Pete. She grabs people by the what's-its and whirls them round faster than a dervish. Two more weeks of her, son, and you'll be needing a retread."

I'll take my chance.

"You what?" Ron guessed Luke's thoughts. "You think she's worth it?"

The gates were open. "Welcome to Wynster-on-Waste."

Ron was too busy to hear. The barge throbbed forward through the first lock gate, nudging close against the second. "Now shut her up, Joshua, and keep those handsome muscles of yours flexed." Ron surveyed the scene, impressed. "Ah, bell-iss-imo! Just like a painting by Poussin: a golden sunset, an uncanny blue light shed beneath the trees – a magic invocation of the ancient pagan world, full of naked gods and goddesses dancing across the greensward!"

Luke glanced about him. "Girl guides are on Tuesdays."

At least Ron was in a better mood than the last time they met. A token of this (not so much Poussin as Pricerite) stood within easy reach on the barge roof – a half-drunk bottle of Hungarian red. Canal merged with river, heading in a gracious circle for River Meadow below the town.

"Now, to decide where goes what. We'll put tents up there, next to the – what trees are they?"

"Aspen."

"Then we'll have the bell tent beside the aspen, and over there, sideshows." Ron had poured out a cup of wine for Luke. He was scanning the meadow. "It's a showman's dream – perfect for what we want. Not too open to make folks hunger for cosy corners, but with enough slope so everybody can see."

Luke was pleased at Ron's response. He had never pictured River Meadow as a theatre. For him it was like a green sea washing against the sea wall of the town, green against limestone grey. He pointed out the Old Schoolhouse where Vera had taught the juniors. "Charles Wesley led hymn-singing up there, and the crowd stretched back to the river."

Ron asked, "Will the audience be on chairs or Mother Earth?"

"Mother Earth. Last time Dad allowed chairs into the open, two thirds disappeared, including about forty in the river."

"Right, speed these around." Ron heaved on to the bank some thirty red and white traffic cones. "Symbols of Britain, Luke. Millions of them, blocking roads from Oakhampton to the Mull of Kintyre ... We'll make a stage-square of poles strung with coloured lights. At each corner there'll be a jumbo lantern, two by the proscenium, two on board *The Lucky Dragon*. The Foghorns want lanterns everywhere."

Ron finished off the wine. "So let's hear about our dear Petra. What's she been up to without Mother Superior Adrienne to rope her to her prayer stool?"

"Just researching. And writing."

"No fights? No arrests for unwomanly conduct?"

"Nothing much. Except that she's found out – we've found out – they're dumping nuclear waste in them thar hills."

Ron screwed up his face. "Impossible. It must be something else." He peered at the ground then fixed Luke with a curious stare. "Tell me about it." He heard a full account of their discovery in Furmiston, though Luke omitted details of exactly how he and Petra had got through the fence.

If need be, I could blame the pine cone.

"Then that explains why Pete's in London – sniffer-dogging up the backsides of the nuclear power mafia. Is she crazy?"

Luke tried to be casual. "We'll not need to go anywhere near Furmiston again."

Ron had begun to splutter like a Chinese firecracker, which was appropriate because he was shifting a large box of fireworks on to the shore. "Let me be clear about one thing, Mr Whistleblower. Am I correct in assuming that while you two know what *they're* up to, they don't know what *you're* up to? Please tell me I'm right."

"Well . . . We've had a bit of a warning."

"They saw you – suspect you?"

Flustered, realising he had been unwise to confide in Ron, Luke answered, "We've promised Dad – or I've promised him, and on Pete's behalf, that we'll . . . keep a low profile from now on."

"Low profile?" Ron stacked the fireworks. "Pete the Mouth – a low profile? She's no more capable of keeping a low profile than the bloody Himalayas. I mean, what do you expect from a Kent miner's daughter? They don't breath air, they breath fire, mate. Look at her hair – that one's descended from the Pictish hordes that ate uncooked Romans for breakfast.

"The only safe place for them was to stick 'em down the coalmines. Course, what did they start doing? They formed unions, preached insurrection, spread the word. Poor pit owners! Then somebody got the bright idea of weeding out the redheads and putting them on a wagon for Dover. Didn't work – those damned Picts dyed their hair with boot-blacking and applied for jobs in the new Kent pits."

Luke responded, "Since when they've been hacking their way towards Westminster carrying the Red Flag."

Ron permitted himself a pale smile, but he was not to be distracted from his panic. "She's putting everybody at risk, Luke. Our Pete doesn't see matters in shades of grey. Things are right or things are wrong. This nuclear power business – for her it'll be totally wrong, but is it that simple? Giving up nuclear power, I mean?"

"There's coal, hundreds of years of it."

"Which causes acid rain that kills off the forests and – "

"What if they used all the money they've poured into nuclear stations to research ways of stopping the pollution?"

Ron backed off from the argument. "Why should I care? After all, they're going to blow the world to bits whatever any of us does."

Luke was out for a better answer than this. "I really want to know what you think, Ron."

"I've told you."

"I could walk under a bus tomorrow, but it doesn't stop me thinking and worrying about things today. Tell me!"

"I don't believe in telling anybody anything." Luke

107

waited, eyes on Ron's face, willing him to answer. "Okay
. . . Look around you. Can you trust mankind not to fuck
things up? Human error – that's why I'm against tampering
with radiation. Human error. Human greed. Human stupidity. It was one human error at Chernobyl – and what
happened? Hundreds of square miles poisoned for centuries. *You* could have inhaled enough radiation from that
disaster to start you off with cancer. And what if you do
die of it, in five years or ten years – how will your dad or
your friends be able to prove it?"

"Then why do people go on saying it's safe?"

"Because their wealth's tied up in it, or their job, or
their prestige, or they're too bloody frightened to tell the
truth. Most of all, because they believe mankind can be
made perfect. All that's required is the right machinery . . .
Now Luke, that's my last word. I don't want to discuss it
any more. Understand?"

Ron stopped to pick up the empty wine bottle. He
hurled it high into the trees. It crashed through the
shimmering silver and plopped into the river.

"Ron," said Luke, with the gentlest hint of reproach,
"that bottle could have hit an innocent fish. Even a carp
full of tadpoles has a right not to suffer concussion from
an Iron Curtain wine bottle."

The words calmed Ron. "Sorry . . . The Sisters get
used to me flying off the handle. It's just, well, that
kid spells disaster." He cupped his hands to his mouth:
"Sorry, carp!" Then he opened his hands and placed his
head in them. "Oh hell. I could see it coming. Trouble!
What do they call this place, Luke?"

"Wynster Bridge."

Now he recalled, took notice. "Wynster-on-Waste –
you said that?"

"Yes."

"I wish I'd never heard of the place."

Chapter 6

"I'm not leaving till the train goes." Always the same, Lena: must wave her loved ones out of sight. A great sister. Thirty pounds in Petra's pocket also speaks of Lena's generosity. "You're all the family we've got left, Midge. Take special care."

All day, Petra had been head down, scribbling. "Tell Adrienne, I don't mind how many alterations she makes . . . just to keep the story."

Reading the first draft of Pete's play, Lena had been impressed. "You've a gift all right." She had agreed to take the script on her prison visit to the Siren Sisters. "I'll slip the sheets between the *Daily Telegraph*. Nobody suspects a *Telegraph* reader."

"Love to Adrienne; love to Ruthy and Luce and Amy. They'll understand why I didn't turn up myself. Some free country when you can't visit your pals in prison without having a spy practically up your dinkum."

Of last night's mystery phone call, followed by the coded threat played on the door bell, and the note warning her that though there might be a tomorrow there might not be a day after, Petra had said nothing.

I have to get out from under Lena's feet before the Ramboids, whoever they are, start picking on her too.

The train from St Pancras was packed. London was being scooped clean by the Friday night exodus. A cannibals' cauldron couldn't have been more uncomfortable than this city of baked potatoes. So many sweating bodies, we could melt the South Pole. What I'd give to be buried up to my neck in ice.

The Wynster would do.

Tight-collared commuters sponging away sweat; visitors on cheap day returns, bunged up with shopping, emptying cans of coke and pineapple which they'd actually bought as gifts for their children; all knackered by the heat which seemed to be solidifying. Vitrified, thought Petra, like tons of waste trapped in glass. All liquidising at the corners.

Is that safe, Professor Schutzman? Unless there's a severe rise in temperature and pressure. That's this carriage at the moment, Prof. Then devitrification takes place.

Melting?

Absolutely – that's the problem. Equally, crystalline ceramics suffer similar effects when they come into contact with brine. Salt sweat: I'm surrounded with it.

"I've three brothers and they all left this country in disgust." Among the witnesses to this sudden outburst as the train brakes were released and the crushed passengers jolted backwards, was Petra herself; no less amazed than her silent listeners. Not an expression changed. It was as if she hadn't spoken.

This provoked her: "And why? Because the place is poisoned from top to bottom."

Again, not a flicker of recognition: she's mad, a redhaired junkie – and what's worse, she has got herself a window seat facing the engine. A last blown kiss from Lena; a mother-manipulated wave from an indifferent Michael. Goodbye Piccadilly, goodbye Leicester Square. Luke Waller and Wynster Carnival, here we come.

Okay, so they think I'm mad. Petra addressed her vitrified audience one last time: "There is no such thing as safe radioactive storage. Yet nobody cares a bugger." Hush, they'll pull the cord, put you off the train. Am I actually slipping off my rocker? Hyperactive, Sam called me. Spinning top, that's me. A scientific miracle defying the laws of nature. Do my feet ever touch the ground?

Try to sleep: it's been a fagging trip. But the brain's a hydraulic ram. Incandescent. Frightening word. Think of the sky – Luke's blue heaven, and let it float.

Like a crane hook?

First stop, Luton. Air from the open doors as the commuters disembarked. Coolant air. Bring back the Ice Age. Petra discovered space to spread. Opposite, a newcomer, concealed behind the *Standard*. The front page headline read.

HEAT CAUSES EARTH TREMORS IN MIDLANDS AND NORTH

She peered closer: fractured gas and water mains in Loughborough; a roof collapse in Salford; two roads fissured and traffic diverted in Sheffield. She could not read more because her companion turned to the sports page.

Petra smiled. There was no getting away from it – the county cricket match between Leicestershire and Glamorgan had been halted, and the headline stated:

'QUAKE STOPS PLAY

Trust the sports page to exaggerate. Personally I'd prefer to report on football. They've all got such terrific legs.

And if the leadmines in Furmiston Forest should suffer an earth tremor; if the fissures opened? Another incident for the play.

Petra felt something touch her hair. She half turned. A cherry stone fell on the ground beside her. A moment later, a second cherry stone hit the window. Thinking it was a kid, and always having had a lot of sympathy for people who had to clean up other people's mess, she lurched round.

"Do you mind?" The words were out before she realised she was addressing two grown men, one Italian-looking, swarthy, handsome. He was smartly dressed in red slacks and a deep blue, open-necked shirt decorated around the collar and down the chest buttons: the cherry-eater.

The second man seemed to be kitted out from Oxfam, in tailor-made cast-offs of high quality, but not quite the right fit. Oxfam, Gerrard's Cross, that is. He sported thickly-sprouting sideburns of not easily defined colour. He was smoking even though this was a No Smoking carriage.

The Italian answered: "Mind what, lady?"

"With the cherry stones."

He held the bag towards her. "You want cherry? They beautiful like your hair."

"No thanks. And I'd rather not have the cherry stones either." Abrupt, but what else could I say? She turned back. Now what?

Bedford, and the carriage was half empty. The truth is, I'm really looking forward to seeing Badgerville again. I feel like Christmas Eve. Perhaps I'm a country girl at the core. With a bit of a fix on a country boy.

"Do you mind?" Her own words turned back on her. Cheekburns was standing over her, dropping cigarette ash on her knee. "Too draughty near the door. My friend suffers from sciatica – don't you, Luigi?"

There are no draughts on these air-conditioned trains.

"I suffer very sigh-attica." The Italian pretended to locate a pain in his side; rubbed it. "Che misero, eh?" His hand passed from the side to the front. He massaged his thigh. "But the pain – I laugh – ha! ha! Vero, Clark?"

Clark?

"True, Luigi. You laugh at the pain."

The Italian sat beside Petra. He thrust the bag of cherries under her nose. "You understand the pain, signorina?"

112

The train was in motion once more, and so were the alarm bells in Petra's head. Are these just a couple of pests – sexual pests – or could their presence be more sinister? You shouldn't have drawn attention to yourself, and put up with the missiles. On the other hand, if these *are* the blokes from the Sierra last night, what difference would it make?

Thankfully I'm not alone.

There was a couple opposite. Yet the man was immersed in the *Financial Times* and the woman deep in a paperback on old English cookery. I've got to say something. Adrienne's advice: back off and you show them you're timid. So what do you do, shout the odds and get your face stoved in?

Use your brains.

The carriage door, engine-end, had opened. Petra acted the instant she saw the ticket inspector. She gathered her yellow and black barrel bag from against her feet and stepped stiffly past Luigi's knees.

"Guard!" She was round Cheekburns' seat. They call it a high-risk decision. "These men are bothering me . . . I'd like to sit somewhere else, please."

"Bothering you, miss?" The ticket inspector was just what Petra needed in a high-risk situation: he was not much taller than the seats, had all the grey hair and wrinkles of a grandfather, and wore a pair of half-moon rimless spectacles on the end of his nose. Yet he did his duty. "Well, gentlemen?"

The gentlemen were an advertisement for unblemished innocence. Sciatica spoilt the scene with an overwrought gesture. "Che magari! This day, you give girl the smile and she shout – penalty, eh?"

Cheekburns soothed: "A domestic quarrel, Officer. Luigi here – they're engaged."

"Certo – engaged. La mia fidanzata." Luigi tried to grasp Petra's arm.

113

"I've never seen these jokers before in my life."

Cheekburns stood up, demonstrating how much taller and wider he was than the ticket inspector. "You hear this, Dad – she's one of us. She's called Petra Scales and she belongs right here."

Petra fought to control her temper, and to stave off panic. "Inspector, these men want locking up! In the meantime, I demand protection." She glanced at the couple opposite. They were hidden behind glass. Vitrified. Eyes riveted into their pages. "Thanks," she said, "for your support."

No response. And it was this rather than Luigi and Cheekburns which triggered Petra's anger. She shouted in the ear of the man locked in the fall-out shelter of the *Financial Times*:

"Am I talking too loud?"

"Sit down, sir." Small and tender he might have been, but the ticket inspector was on home ground. "Sit down or I shall have to ask for further assistance."

"Free country, eh?" protested Luigi. "You call thees free country?"

"Yes," barked back Petra, "free for molesters and *Financial Times* readers!"

"Now young lady – "

Cheekburns: "You tell her, pal – "

Ticket inspector: "And you tell Romeo here that this is British Rail."

The Italian's sunny mood vanished. For a split second the world seemed to stand utterly still; and when it slipped into motion again, the air was freezer-cold, and so menacing that Cheekburns acted to check his friend even though, as yet, Luigi had taken no action.

"Okay, Luigi – no sweat, eh? Not here. Right?" Cheekburns gripped his friend above the elbow, held the arm at his side. "Orders, Luigi – va bene?"

Petra insisted, "I'm not staying in this compartment."

114

"She can sit by me, Inspector." A woman near the forward door; blonde, good-looking, but severe. In these circumstances, reassuring. Petra hesitated.

The ticket inspector was anxious to settle things. "All right, miss?"

She was uneasy but – well, women together. It's got to be better than wandering up and down the train alone. Petra assented.

"I'm Stacey."

"Petra."

"Yobs."

They were more than that, but Petra merely nodded. "You never get used to it, do you?"

"Like hell not." Stacey was tall. Her hair was drawn tightly back from her forehead and pinned in a bunch behind her. Very businesswoman-like: fawn suit, pleated skirt – what was it Ruthy said about women in pleated skirts? Can't remember. And a mauve silk blouse with matching bow-tie. "We could go next door, Petra. They'll not bother us there."

"I'd prefer that."

The inspector escorted them to a new seat in a new carriage. "If they come through that door," Petra threatened, "I'm pulling the cord."

Stacey had her firmly by the wrist. "Just stiffs. It's over now – relax."

Petra sat facing the far door. She was angry, afraid. It's not over yet. She clutched her briefcase to her chest. One foot was stuck in territorial defiance on her barrel bag. "They know my name."

Stacey was motherly, coaxing. "That, my dear, is because it's written on your bag." She laughed. She was not quite so poised as she seemed at first. Perhaps Petra's tension was contagious. Anyway, Stacey's also taking a risk. It might be her turn next time.

They were sitting opposite an American couple. The man, in his early sixties, wore a tartan golf cap. His wife sported ornate magenta-tinted spectacles with a gold safety chain. They were leafing through a booklet entitled *Our British Heritage*.

"Here comes coffee – want some, Petra?"

"My treat, for the rescue."

Stacey smiled appreciatively. "Women have got to stick together, right?"

Right? What is it that's making me feel all isn't right? It came to mind what Ruthy had actually said: never trust a woman in pleats. Very mean-minded, and ungrateful.

"How far are you travelling, Petra?" asked Stacey, as the steward poured coffee into plastic cups and Petra offered payment.

"Well, not all the way." What sort of answer is that?

"North?"

"Sort of." Safety in numbers, Dad had always said. Or was it strength in numbers? Either way, Stacey mustn't get the idea I'm in her pocket. Petra raised her cup to the Americans. "Not as good as your American coffee."

"You bin to the States, young lady?" The couple were glad of this sudden contact from the usually taciturn English traveller.

"My sister Gabrielle's out there. Married. Her kids talk with accents halfway between Chatham and Cincinnati."

"That is my wife Minnie, and I'm Harry." The American shot out his hand to Petra who grasped it, and passed it on to Stacey who was not expecting it. "My sister lives three hundred miles from nowhere – a place called Spokane, ever heard of it?"

Harry shook his head. "It's a big country."

"I was out there for a month. Gabby was so homesick, she'd drive up to Canada just to buy Bovril and proper English biscuits. Not that she particularly liked Bovril."

The American couple were stopping off shortly to visit Minnie's cousin Eve. Then they planned to travel on to York. "Great city, eh? Real England, the book says."

For an instant, Petra shifted her gaze from the suntanned good cheer of Harry to the end of the carriage. Cheekburns and Luigi had come out of their own carriage and stood by the lavatories. They were staring in Petra's direction; watching, waiting.

Luigi even waved, once more proffered cherries. He stepped towards the automatic door which obediently opened for him. Petra jerked back in her seat. Luigi grinned, stepped clear, and the door shut once more.

Cat and mouse, Miss Scales.

Stacey had joined in the conversation. She was saying how much she admired America. "Your president is such a sweetie."

Inside, Petra curled up: 'Sweetie' was the last word she would have used to describe the current president of the United States.

"I don't recommend York," she said, more sharply than she intended. "It's chocolate-box, full of antique shops. Nothing at all like the Britain most of us have to live in." Her voice carried down the compartment. She preferred it that way.

Safety in numbers, Dad.

"Why not try Liverpool instead? That's real Britain. There's not much of it still standing, so you'd better hurry. My friend Luce was born there. Brought up in Toxteth where there's a national holiday every time somebody gets a job."

"I don't think I want to see Liverpool, Harry."

"Then why not Cornwall? My friend Amy's from there. Very beautiful."

"Yeah?"

Stacey was glancing at the compartment door. Petra felt

a surge of terror because her instinct told her, as much as her eyes, that Stacey had given Cheekburns and Luigi a meaningful look. Keep out, it seemed to say. Petra caught their response: they nodded – or is it my imagination? And then they turned their backs.

Anyone would think you knew them, Stacey.

She suppressed her fears with words, warning the Americans about exploring Cornwall: "But see you don't go near the old china-clay mines. They're hot!"

"Hot?"

"Course they closed them down ages ago ... weird places. I performed in a play down there last year. Everything's ghostly white. As if all the colour in the world had drained away. Deep in the mineshafts, they've started to sink ..." She raised her voice, projected it: "Nuclear waste – "

"Y'mean dumped it? That stuff's mighty dangerous."

"Naturally they've fenced the caves off for miles around. Stuck armed guards all over the place. A few witnesses disappear from time to time, but what's that compared to the cash the Japanese will pay to get shot of the stuff?"

"But is it safe?"

"Oh yes. Unless it leaks. In which case the white clay turns russet colour, and then scarlet. That's when the earth starts to smoulder."

"Good God, that sounds as bad as that Russian disaster – "

"Chernobyl?"

"Yes."

"Or your own Three Mile Island." Petra clamped her hand on Stacey's wrist. "Know anything about Three Mile Island, Stacey?"

Stacey stared at Petra. Hard. She disengaged her hand. "Why should I?"

"Well, there are a lot of people in and around my life at the moment who keep dark secrets."

"Sorry?"

"It's no secret," said Harry. "We're from Wisconsin, so we were a long ways from the danger. But that damned nuclear station nearly blew to high heaven."

"Exactly how was that, Harry?"

"Don't recall the details, o'course."

"The reactor rods got uncovered, didn't they? The coolant didn't do its job."

"You kinda read up on these things?"

"And a large hydrogen bubble was created – correct? Two days later, out shoots a plume of radioactive gas, blowing in the direction of Middleton."

"Middleton, yeah. I remember the name."

"And like at Chernobyl, the area had to be evacuated . . . My dad was a miner. They're for shutting his old pit down."

"I guess nuclear power must be cheaper than coal," thought Harry."

"Not a bit of it. The power stations are a front to produce bombs." Petra's voice detonated almost with the power of a nuclear device. "If they didn't want the bombs they wouldn't need the plutonium. And if they didn't need the plutonium they would not have to reprocess spent fuel, which is the horribly dangerous bit."

The train was slowing: a major station.

"They can make waste safe," ventured Stacey. "It's an accepted fact. The worst thing you can do is get all emotional about it."

"Safe as houses?"

"Yes."

"And if there's an earthquake, where are the safe houses?"

Stopping. Petra's change; the Americans' change. Safety

in numbers, Dad. "Thanks, Stacey, you've been a real pal."
Up, helping Minnie with her case. "I'll carry this for you.
Mine's only got clothes in – and a geiger counter." She
clasped Stacey's hand, leant over her, against her, making
sure she did not get up. "I'll go ahead, Harry, and open
the door."

"That's very kind of you, young lady."

"Pete to my friends."

People were alighting from the rear of the carriage.
They blocked any pathway Cheekburns and Luigi might
have been hoping for. They had to retreat to let passengers
out.

Petra could not see Stacey. I've probably done her
wrong. At least I was polite. Apart from tipping her and
suggesting she'd look nicer in jumpers than blouses, what
could I do?

On the platform, glancing round, trying not to
hurry Minnie and Harry along; yet aware that the train
would be stopped for a while, for unloading and load-
ing.

Plenty of faces, none recognisable, thank God. So far,
so good. Towards the platform stairs. Up, over, down, and
along to the main exit. "Harry, would you do me a favour?
I'd like to make a phone call, and I'd appreciate it if you
could just, well – stand guard."

"Surely, Pete. These draughty places are not always
safe as houses for young ladies. Specially pretty ones."

"Thanks ... Minnie, if you see that Stacey, would
you let me know?"

"Right ... Isn't she your friend?"

Petra closed the phonebox door. Beware of women
in pleated skirts.

Luke was sitting in a deckchair just outside the kitchen
door, sweltering by moonlight. He answered the phone.

"Luke Waller – oh, Pete, great ... Not great?" He listened. He frowned. "No, not Wynster, Pete. They'll have somebody waiting. Get off at Rowmanton. You're straight off the platform into the car park. I'll be there."

Alfred: "Let me speak to her."

"It's not Vera, Dad." As Luke replaced the phone he remembered – too late – that it was the down platform that led directly out into the car park. Pete will have to go over the bridge. If she's not careful she'll come out the wrong side. Idiot!

"What's the matter, Luke?"

"That was Pete. She's got company ... And I've just given her lousy instructions."

The face-slap saved Petra; or the sound of it. The Wynster train left from platform six. That meant recrossing the bridge. Then the slap, and Petra lunged back. She ducked under the staircase.

Luigi the striker, Stacey the struck. "Peesed it up, you bitch? How we peesed it up?"

"Because you couldn't resist the skirt, could you?"

"We had her," remonstrated Cheekburns.

"You lost her!"

"*You* bloody lost her, not us."

"Why didn't you keep quiet as per Don's instructions?"

Through the iron grille of the stairs, Petra could see three figures descending.

"You is nobody but the cheap skirt yourself," barked Luigi. "Signor Neeson – "

"Don't you 'Signor Neeson' me, Luigi. For somebody wanted for terrorism in his own country, you make a big noise – "

"Okay, okay, break it up," commanded Cheekburns, playing the part of Mr Sweet Reason. "What do we do now?"

Luigi: "I screw the redhead when I catch her!"

"You'll do what you're paid to do ... If the kid's any sense," said Stacey, "she'll keep out of sight till the last second. Then she'll hop out on to the Wynster Bridge train."

"If there're corridors, we've got her."

"We take her at Wynster, not before."

"Sure, Stacey – you're the boss." Cheekburns proposed they go for a drink. "We've half an hour to kill."

Stacey agreed. "But listen – she's sharp, so next time don't go at her like bulls at a gate. Capisci, Luigi? Understand?"

Petra almost warmed to Stacey. Slapped across the face she might have been, but she reasserted herself. She was in charge.

So Luigi is wanted for terrorism. Nice one, Don.

Tarndale, Heatherbridge, Priestley Bottom, then Rowmanton. Petra acknowledged her luck: no corridor on the train, and some company – an elderly lady returning from her son's in the south. Cuddly, plump, like Mum before she faded and shrivelled with her illness. Wide-faced, full of life and bustle, listing the signposts in the life of her wonderful offspring; yet somehow not boastful. I'd like somebody to talk about me like this, just now and then.

Heatherbridge, and Petra helped the lady out with her case, its handle secured with a fleecy blue ribbon. "Your son sounds like a really nice person," she said. "Because he strikes me as having a really nice mum."

She waved goodbye. She was alone. Her pulses were playing Heavy Metal now: will they guess? And even if they don't, will I be able to cover the ground fast enough?

If Luke's ten seconds late . . .

She rehearsed her escape. Don't get out till the train's about to move. The car park will be straight off the platform. Priestley Bottom. She sat away from the window.

Rowmanton next stop: what did they mean, 'take me'?

Check: barrel bag, with clothes and camera; and first draft of the play hidden in a cylindrical biscuit box, macaroons to be precise. Check: Lena's briefcase, with a fact-packed diary and a wadge of information on the dumping of nuclear waste. Check: one shaking body, comprising oven-dry mouth, sweat-shining nose, cracked lips and numb feet.

Approaching Rowmanton, slowing: tunnel through Castle Hill. Heart banging. Hand on the window, waiting. Hold it, hold it. Stopped. Only a few passengers alighting. Not yet, wait for the whistle. Wait. She thrust down the window. Still she waited. Come on, come on.

The whistle went.

"Christ! – she's getting off here!"

The train was moving.

"Out, then!"

Doorbang followed doorbang. Petra running, barrel bag swinging. Looked ahead along the platform: no car park. Instead, a major road. She almost halted in confusion. She forgot everything. They were out, behind her. Cheekburns and Luigi got in each other's way, but the chase was on, leaving Stacey rocking on high heels.

Petra passed a woman pulling a shopper. "Car park – please!"

"Over."

She saw the bridge. She sprinted. "Sorry!" She bundled past a couple with suitcases.

"What's the rush?"

Petra was up the steps, forcing her way past two more passengers. The pursuers were slowed at the bottom of the stairs.

"Permesso!" yelled Luigi: and who'd understand that?

"Gangway!" roared Cheekburns.

"Look, what's the—?"

"Police!"

Making it. Petra went down the steps, all clear, in twos. The rails flashed beneath her. Ahead, the valley, cleft between monster hills. The sky had exploded with stars. She hit the horizontal. They were above, among the stars, calling. She half turned. A mistake, for she bumped into a passenger heading for the steps.

Lena's briefcase was gone. It slithered to the edge of the platform. "Hell!" They were racing down. No option. Leave it. Oh Christ – my diary; everything!

"Excuse me, miss." The passenger had stopped for the briefcase. He was burgeoned off it by Luigi and Cheekburns.

"We'll give it to her, mate. You get the train."

The ticket collector also wanted to know why the hurry. Petra stuffed her ticket into his hand. "Buses?"

"No buses. Here!"

Out into the car park, at first blind to everything but what the eye in the back of her head was telling her.

"Pete!" Luke was on the pavement under the glass canopy, facing the exit, engine screaming for action.

She straddled, gripped. "I've lost my diary! Those buggers!"

The Navigator cut a half circle through its own exhaust smoke.

Ticket collector: "Hey-up, what's the . . ? Tickets, gentlemen!"

"Bloody hell, she's on that bike!"

"These are for Wynster, sir. And that's the last – "

"We prefer the air here."

"Now that I can't credit, gentlemen. Wynster Bridge is famous for its . . . ." The men crashed past him, out into the car park. ". . . It's, er, champagne air."

"I dropped my case!" yelled Petra, but the sound of

124

the Navigator, the barrier of his helmet, the tension and his own cry of relief, deafened Luke.

All his senses were in his eyes. He aimed straight for the station entrance. He slapped the Norton's petrol tank in affection. "Silver, the Wonder Horse!"

Luigi and Cheekburns were left stranded – but only for a few moments. The instant the Norton turned off into the traffic, a green Escort slipped into the station car park.

Sandy: "Want a lift, chaps?"

Luigi: "You from - ?"

Paddy: "Yeah, we're from. Hop in. Where's the boss's girl?"

"She bloody disastro!"

"Shsh, Luigi," cautioned Cheekburns. "Your voice carries." Stacey was crossing the forecourt. She was presented with Petra's briefcase. "How about this for a Chrissy present for Mr Neeson? And it's real leather."

Upper town deserted. Road beaming up to the sky, stopped from dashing straight into the Milky Way by the ruined keep on Castle Hill, walls propped up with scaffolding.

"I've lost my briefcase, Luke."

The driver heard nothing. "Beautiful. And just glad to see you." "It had my diary in it." "I've got the boot from Monarch. It's closing down next month." "Luckily I put the play in my bag." "Tears all round this morning. Even Grizzly Gifford." "All my notes on waste . . . and description of the slides I took." "Yes, they'll be ready by Wednesday." "Those bastards will know everything, Luke. Everything we've been up to."

"The good news is your Siren-cum-Foghorns are released on Monday."

"I think there's a car wanting to overtake, Luke."

Shouting in the wind: "I've been pretty useless without you, Pete." "An Escort, Luke." Up the first leg of Switchback, crookedest section of road in Britain, everything reaching inwards, nearly touching.

One in eight.

"Luke!"

"But now I feel over the moon ... Ron's arrived. He's borrowed Bill Gordon's car to fetch them up."

"They want to overtake, Luke."

The Escort was so close behind them that it was amazing Luke had not spotted them in his mirror. He speeded up. The road switched back in accord with its reputation. Up and left, levelling, climbing again.

And bump.

Now Luke noticed. "They've hit us." He was fighting for control. Up on the verge, along it, brushing a dry-stone wall. Still going. He signalled them to overtake.

"Luke," bellowed Petra. "They want *us!*"

At last brain and eye worked together: the green Escort, a shadow no longer.

Bump – a sidewards blow, sending Luke off tarmac once more, over and into a low ditch. He yanked the bars, followed the ditch, pulled out and just managed to stay ahead.

They were front wheel to back wheel, and the Escort was swinging to ram. Luke accelerated, avoided collision. But there was no more sprint left in the Navigator.

A car coming in the opposite direction forced the Escort to drop back. Luke took his chance. He went head down, with Petra head down behind him, taking the bend as only two wheels can.

Another car, and another second in Luke's favour.

Then – "Oh no!" In front, on a short, steep incline, a tractor pulling a ton of hay. It was almost stopped halfway up the hill. Two tons of hay. Whatever the weight, the trailer was overloaded. "At this time of night?"

The tractor was square in the middle of the road, permitting less than a yard on either side. Luke almost hit the rear-light of the trailer as he sensed the Escort against his own rear-light.

"He's drunk!" decided Petra, as the tractor veered left then giddily to the right.

Tractor and load dipped into a shallow ditch, hit the banking and three hay bales were shed on to the verge, a fourth on to the road. Over came the load, down came two more bales.

Luke was waiting for a gap — but which side, and would the drunken driver opt to change tack at the last second?

Another bale missed them by inches. Not so lucky, the Escort. It had to brake hard and pull round the offending hay. Luke waited, eye to light, eye to tail. Now — he went through, between tractor and wall.

The Escort nosed after, but the tractor driver had finally decided it was safer on the left-hand side of the road. He swung his trailer across the bonnet of the Escort.

The two vehicles didn't so much meet head to tail as play sandwiches with the roadside wall. The hay mountain was no more. It was decapitated into a modest range of foothills. Its proud peak now capsized all over the Escort.

The hay struck and burst. It split itself over windscreen, open sunroof, windows, blinding the occupants with the pungent odour of the countryside. The Escort slid up the bank. It hit a surface somewhat more substantial than a hay bale.

But not that substantial.

The five foot wall atop a four foot bank had, it seems, been waiting for months or years for this final humiliation to compound ages of neglect. In short, one stone fell and then, like the hay bales, all the wall fell.

Petra glanced back on the scene of rustic chaos as Luke swept up the far hill. The occupants of the Escort were out, cursing and inspecting the damage, fist-waving at the tractor driver who, oblivious to the mayhem he had caused, orbited right into a farm lane.

Still singing his head off, he vanished into a powdery darkness.

Luke and Petra celebrated the moment. Somehow, she thought, we'll get blamed, but for the present she clutched Luke and shouted to the heavens:

"Victory!"

Chapter 7

In the centre of the grey raked gravel, Luke's Japanese garden, there was an intruder: a single blossom had fallen from the upper garden, and now lodged scarlet and still at the foot of the limestone rock; the little Mellport Stone.

For minutes on end, Luke had stared at the blossom, his mind searching for reasons to explain why he was suddenly cast down. Was it Ron? "Admit it, Luke," Ron had said before departing south to pick up the Siren Sisters, "you're shit-scared. And you don't need me to warn you somebody's likely to get killed."

Thanks, Ron, for spoiling a perfect morning.

So still, so hot. You lift a hand and out pours a bucket of sweat. The hills are the colour of underdone toast. The church bell broke the silence, a hesitant chime, summoning worshippers more in hope than expectation.

I ought to be bouncing; steaming with joy. Last night they had stopped at the Frost Demon. They had kissed and when they had come home, Petra had abandoned her own room for Luke's. "It's about time."

You're stunned, that's all. Not surprising. Even now, was it a dream? You're on edge because all at once you want to stop time, go through each second, like precious jewels; yet time's a runaway truck with no brakes. It's crashing downhill with a load of nuclear waste. It'll come right through the house and knock your love-match for six.

Before I can think.

There was another shadow on the future. Last night, Petra had said, "Join the Siren Sisters, Luke. Join the

129

world." He had raised his eyes to it, and the world terrified him. The world without all this, without Alfred. Time to leave the tribe, Luke. To prove yourself, to be free.

In a week, she would be gone. He would have to decide. She would be gone – and then what silence there'll be; solid as limestone; dark as the Frost Demon when it blocks out the sun.

"Does it ever cross your mind to ask me to stay with you, Luke Waller?"

"It's never out of my mind, but – "

"But what, if I . . . really care about you?"

"Who called Wynster a living death?"

"Maybe I've changed."

"You without the Sisters, me without a job?"

He knew he had disappointed her. "You always see the dark side first." I need more time, Pete – but will there be enough?

The last thing Luke expected to happen to the time he had left with Petra was for it to be wasted in a quarrel; and result in a painful separation. But it happened.

Alfred had announced a surprise: "The Carnival Committee and helpers have got together to put on a welcome for the Siren Sisters. Nothing fancy – bangers, sausage rolls, ice-buns and a firkin of ale; with a promise from Councillor Hartfield, our chairman, to desist from speech making – if that's at all possible."

Ron was due back with four ex-guests of Holloway Prison – Adrienne, Ruth, Luce and Amy – by mid-evening. The word had gone out: open house at the Wallers; just like old times when Vera threw parties like handfuls of confetti.

By seven-thirty, Church Hall was as packed as Bingo Night. Wynster Athletic, first and second teams, had come after a practice match; the all-woman picket at the Ecclestone's factory had downed placards and decided to take time off from a protest which had stretched from last October, when wage-cuts had been imposed on the workforce; all Luke's workmates from Monarch were there, with sundry spouses and offspring; the tennis courts and cricket nets had been deserted, mid-session, at the news of free beer; even a passing cohort of ramblers wandered in. They were full of questions about what had happened to the public footpath through Furmiston Forest. "We got slagged off like nobody's business."

"And all that shooting."

"Shooting?"

"There'll not be a bird or an animal left alive up there, if it goes on."

Connie Hillsmore, last of the suffragettes, in whose garden Luke had been away labouring most of the afternoon and evening, button-holed Petra near the Japanese garden. "I've a bone to pick with you, my dear." She was all smiles. "Somebody has definitely cast a spell on our Luke. He mowed straight through a bed of marigolds this afternoon and then fell through my new trellis. He's either on drugs or in love ... Now we can't afford to lose the best gardener for miles around. He should go to horticultural college. It's his gift, and somebody round here ought to persuade him."

Connie rounded off by saying that Luke's prowess as a gardener was the only thing she and 'that dratted Councillor Hartfield can ever agree on'. Inside the Church Hall, the said dratted councillor had just been snapped at by his wife for fingering the sausage rolls before the guests of honour arrived. "I was only testing them for freshness, pet."

"Do partake, Councillor, if you're feeling peckish." Alfred set a bad example by downing a small meat pie.

Councillor Hartfield's abiding sensation whenever he talked to Alfred Waller was of suspicion. He sensed he was always being waylaid, sidetracked or led up the garden path by the Red Reverend; usually all three. "I confess, Reverend, to a not inconsiderable anxiety that we're actually celebrating the release of a bunch of criminals."

"Not criminals as such, Councillor. Rather we might describe them as, er, political prisoners."

"Political prisoners in Great Britain? – stuff and nonsense, Vicar. This isn't the Soviet Union."

"Isn't it?" queried Connie wheeling herself into the conversation. "Tell me why it's not the Soviet Union, Noel? Tell me what's become of the difference?"

"Constance, I – "

"They tap our phones. Put electric fences round Britain's loveliest countryside. We can't protest without permission. We can't picket without permission – good heavens, you call this a free country? The only freedom we're left with is to keep our gobs shut."

"Pete, you're shivering."

"Where've you been all day?" She was sitting on the stone bench outside the kitchen window.

"Earning . . . I told you. I'm sorry. It's been a list of disasters. Couldn't concentrate." He sat down beside her. She rested her head on his shoulder. "What's the matter?"

"I'm scared, Luke."

"You, of all people?"

"Suddenly and stupidly scared."

He sensed the reason. "Because of the Sisters coming?"

"Sort of . . . I've made all the running while they've been locked up. I've been free – to make decisions, like doing the play. I got a taste for it, not being junior houseboy any more." She sighed loudly and hunched up her shoulders as though the wind off the moor were practising for winter. "By sticking Furmiston at the heart of the action, I've . . . I've put everybody at risk."

He was silent: it's as if she had only now realised the

danger to everyone in turning the whispers of Furmiston into voices on stage.

"Will they understand, Luke?"

"They'll understand." She expected more. She waited. He said nothing.

"But understanding is only the first thing. The play is asking more than understanding."

"Yes." Again, no embellisment.

She waited, then went on, "It's demanding . . . commitment. Heads on the block, isn't it?"

"Could be."

"You could be more helpful!"

"Sorry. I'm as confused as you are."

"But I'm not confused. Afraid, yes. Scared out of my head, yes – but not confused."

In his own confusion, Luke struggled to do better, give her the reassurance she was hoping for. "Ron will have tried to talk them out of doing the play."

"You know that?"

Luke nodded. "But if the Siren Sisters are what you say they are, they'll listen to Ron – and do just the opposite."

She brightened. "Of course! The more Ron pours cold water, the more the Sisters will . . ." She was still uncertain. "But you, Luke. You seem, well, to be having second thoughts."

"I'm always Mr But, you know that."

"You weren't last night. No if-ing and but-ing there. I want to know whether you're really in this thing with me, that you agree I'm doing the right thing."

Alfred was along the path, and calling: "Come on, you two – they're here!"

Petra leapt up. Luke had things to bring from the house. "I want an answer, Luke Waller."

Doesn't she know by now?

He had a record cleaner to find, and a wedge to stop the stereo wobbling on the uneven hall floor. He was on his way out when the phone rang. For a moment, he thought the voice was Vera's. "Mum?" A slip of the tongue in his delight.

"Who's that speaking, please?" A woman's voice he did not recognise.

"Luke Waller."

"Petra – is she at home?"

"I'll fetch her. She's – "

"Please don't. I've a train to catch. My message is very brief." For a moment the speaker was silent, then: "Are you the boy she writes about in her diary?"

"Look, who is this?"

"Please – no questions, just listen. I'm Stacey Mills. I was Petra's not-very-friendly bodyguard the other night . . . I am out of all this, and I've only a few minutes before my train. I want to warn you – all of you. Petra, Alfred – even Vera."

"Vera? How – "

"In Petra's diary. You're all there. Everything's there. At the moment it's being passed round the billets like a dirty novel. Anyway, that diary . . . it was the most beautiful thing. Perhaps it decided me. I'm leaving. There were a lot of things I'd not realised – she's done her homework.

"All I have to say – are you there?"

"Yes, I'm sorry."

"The men you're tangling with kill for money, and the stakes are now sky high. They're gunning for you, especially Petra . . . Don't talk, just take the advice. The dumping will go on. It's dangerous for the present and disastrous for the future, but it'll go on – not just in your neck of the woods, but everywhere."

Luke: "We agreed not to go back."

There was a crackling on the line. "Cancel the play . . . Can you hear me? Cancel."

"She'll never agree – "

"Cancel it! Don't put the play on. Don't show those slides she writes about. And don't, for Christ's sake, say who gave you this warning." The pips went. No further cash was available, but the message required no further air-time.

A rap on the half-open kitchen door made Luke twist round in fright. "Nigel!"

Mrs Fowles' boy had come for the wedge and record cleaner. "Expecting burglars?"

"You could say that." Luke replaced the receiver.

"Bad news?" Bright boy.

"Oh no."

Nigel grinned. "I'd be feeling pale if she was my girl – your Pete."

"Not *my* Pete."

"Anyway, she's a cracker. Full of bounce. I like 'em," said thirteen-year-old Nigel, "when they've got something to grab hold of."

Stifled by the remorseless heat in the house, Luke went up through the garden. To his left, the moor; right, the iron gate into the sloping cemetery behind the church. He stopped by the stone stile. He stooped to dead-head a bush-rose which, despite the fading light, shone like flames against the grey stone wall. The burning bush. It was a petal from these roses which still lay on the gravel of the Japanese garden.

What do I do?

The breeze off the moor was touched with autumn. Our winter's coming early. Must break the spell. Yet these things . . . the garden's like wax, not made of natural sub-stances at all. Nothing fades, nothing falls. Except the petal.

Everything's right with the world. The flowers say it; the sun, the sky, the horizon – perfect. Nothing changes, that's what the moment seems to say. The world is slow, orderly and in harmony. Perfect . . .

A perfect pretence.

Stacey's call could have been a trick to scare us. But she gave her name. She took a risk. There you go, Pete, touching people again, converting them; even if it's only your lost diary. Can I work this out for all of us? Be absolutely still like the cypress. That's easy enough. Don't move, and you fade into the landscape.

Act, and then what? If I back out on her now, would she ever forgive me? If I let things be, and she gets hurt – will I ever forgive myself?

In Church Hall, the Siren Sisters were unwinding from their astonishment at such a welcome. Nigel's music was rafter-quivering. Over fifty guests had surrounded trestle tables beneath Alfred's largely unremarked mural, stabbing pickles, prodding sausage rolls, dolloping potato salad; most of them electing for Alfred's home-brewed cider in their plastic cups, which didn't waste space on froth, the others licking the top off their beer in order to get an extra mouthful to slake August-parched thirsts.

"Reminds me of the Royal Weddin'," thought Madge; and there was general agreement that people had not got together much lately. "But what's there been to celebrate?" considered Freda. "Bugger all!" concluded Ellen. "Still, these theatre folk should have enough oomph to go round."

Everybody agreed: oomph was what Wynster Bridge needed. Plenty of it. And these real live actresses had good looks to go with the oomph.

"Talkin' of good looks, the Reverend's smartened himself up."

"Poor beggar . . . Not as I blame that Vera. She showed guts, get-up-and-go."

136

"Aye, that Vera had oomph. Her kind of thing, all this – plays, cabaret in the street, dancin' till dawn. You could see it in her eye."

"There's not been much shine in our Luke's eye till lately."

"Don't worry, this Pete'll put some lead in his pencil!"

This Pete was ensconced among the Siren Sisters on the steps up to the Hall stage. Back in the team – it was a great feeling. Arm around her, Adrienne proposed a toast in cider: "Absent friends!" In mind were their allies in the Peace Camps; those still in their benders, eternally watched by the police and their dogs, and those still in jail for crimes of conscience. "To the Peace Women everywhere!"

"And the Peace Men?" queried Ron.

"If there are any," answered Ruth. She prodded Ron, nearly flattening him. "After all, who starts the fighting – women?"

"Helen of Troy caused – "

"Crap. All the Greeks and Trojans needed was an excuse to cut each other's throats and grab the trade routes."

"Remember me, Pete? Len Williams, from BBC Radio Rowmanton."

"Ah, so you've decided I'm not crackers after all."

"I've made a few enquiries about Furmiston, and the other things you told me. I reckon you're on to a good story."

"About Tattershall – anything on him?"

"Not so far. But his son, Lance; there's a trail warming up in that direction."

"Does he drive a Lamborghini?"

Len grinned. "Give me time. Anyhow, I may have a starter to go out in the next couple of days."

"Make it before the Carnival – timing's everything."

"That's fine by me." Len indicated his tape recorder.

"If we could find somewhere quiet, I'd like you and Luke to describe your trip into Furmiston for me."

"Sure – but our best secrets we're keeping for the Carnival play."

"An hors d'oeuvre, then?"

The creaking Hall floor had filled with dancers. Big Luce had been clasped in the arms of Bill Gordon. Her amazing smile beamed down on the balding pate of the diminutive Bill whose entire life had been spent looking up to, and admiring, tall women.

Not entirely the prisoner of his own pomposity, Councillor Hartfield had been tempted by the long flaxen tresses of Adrienne. He tapped her on the shoulder, only for Mrs Hartfield to put a wheel-clamp on his elbow. "Dance, Noel?"

Spluttering as usual, "Oh yes, m'dear – naturellement!"

Alfred proved the lucky partner. Despite the beat of the music which suggested a modicum of go-go, Alfred held Adrienne as if they were doing the modern waltz. "This is a really great day for us, Adrienne. True theatre people in town – protest theatre to boot. Time to shake the place up."

"There may be a spot of trouble, I hear."

"Well, naturally . . . If you fight, you must expect a black eye occasionally."

"Black eyes belong to the past, Reverend."

"Alfred, please . . . Did Vera – my wife – did she visit you . . . inside?"

"Twice. We appreciated it."

"She's good in that way. Er, how is she?"

Adrienne took time to find the right answer. She resisted stating the plain truth, that Vera was happy. "She talks about you . . . And Luke."

"She didn't say whether – ?"

"No second thoughts, Alfred. Not yet."

Alfred changed the subject. "Pete was worried that, her play – "

"That we'd not like it?" He was thinking, a smile like Adrienne's was worth the price of a theatre ticket. "Who can deny Pete anything? We got the script from Lena, her sister. It's good – very funny, and very bitter. So we've rehearsed, and we're ready for off."

"No?"

The voice was a bullet: and the echo of a bullet.

"No?" Petra could not take in what Luke had said. "What do you mean, no?"

He avoided looking into her face. "I'm sorry. I'm not going to do the interview. At least not till after the Carnival's over."

Len mistook Luke's reason for refusing to be taped. "You'll be okay. If you dry up, I'll feed you the right questions. And we can edit out the gaps later."

"It's nothing to do with drying up."

The rift remained bridgeable. Petra's hand closed round Luke's arm. "It'll be all right."

"It won't be all right – I'm not doing it."

"Look at me!"

"We're out of our depth, Pete."

"What are you saying, that we don't . . . that we shut up shop? Shut our mouths?" He felt her go cold on him; felt her dismay; her inability to grasp his change of heart. Perhaps the words they were using meant different things. "What's come over you, Luke?"

"Ladies, gentlemen – and thespians of the world!" Alfred was on stage, calling the gathering to attention. "Just a few words, if I may."

Nigel reduced the volume of the music but kept it running as background, and as a reminder that this wasn't a night for speeches. Noel Hartfield, being chairman of the

139

Carnival Committee, took his place expectantly at the foot of the stage steps. He too had a few words in mind.

Luke stared at Petra, but it was her turn to avert her gaze. He'd put it wrongly. The timing had been hopeless. You dumb oaf. You've blown it. You should have talked to her first, alone; tried to explain; told her about Stacey's warning. Too late now – she won't even look at you.

Alfred: "First, a very warm welcome to a group of young people whose commitment to a safer, better world puts a great many of us of an older generation to shame . . . But we've a splendid opportunity in the next few days to let the Siren Sisters help this community."

"Help *us*?" snorted Councillor Hartfield, more to himself than to the public at large. "I thought we were helping them."

"We in Wynster Bridge," Alfred continued, "have our own chance to speak out for our fellow men and women at next Saturday's Grand Carnival. Our theme of friendship, community and racial harmony has acquired a new dimension in recent days – namely, the growing evidence that our very hills are being poisoned, that strangers from heaven knows where have erected fences patrolled by armed guards. What we all need to ask is – why weren't we told? Why weren't we consulted?"

"Pigs'll fly, Reverend," shouted Madge, "before anybody up there consults the likes of us."

Councillor Hartfield's foot had been tapping with increasing impatience. The Red Reverend was at it again. Now he banged his foot on the bottom step. "Vicar, what's happening up at Furmiston is private business and nothing whatsoever to do with the Wynster Carnival."

Madge, in good voice: "Them leadmines, Councillor, stretch right under this town."

"Nonsense, madam."

"You check your facts, Sir No-all – and I for one refuse

140

to pay my rates to have nuclear waste come bubblin' up my drains!"

"Who the devil said anything about nuclear waste?"

"They're dumpin' somethin' – and they'd not stick miles of expensive fencin' up, would they, if it were just French letters they were stashin' away?"

Laughter. Councillor Hartfield's "Madam!" was drowned in a tide of applause.

"Luke? I'm sorry, I should have warned you." Petra had had time to think things over. Maybe she misunderstood him. Don't be so snappy. We're all on edge. "Len wants just a quick interview – nothing detailed . . . Please!"

I'm numb. With anguish and dread. With terror. I know nothing. I'm another person. And as another person, Luke watched his own reactions: his face was stiff, neck stiff, body stiff; becoming ill with the shock of knowing I'm making it all worse.

He watched his head shake; heard, "I'm sorry, Petra . . . Petra? I'd like to explain."

"Like hell you will!"

"It's too dangerous."

"Then bugger you!" Petra's voice exploded across the hall.

"I beg your pardon?" Noel Hartfield was under the impression that he was the target of this attack.

Petra heard nothing, saw nothing but Luke: Luke blocking her way, Luke letting her down. She barged into him.

"Sod off!"

"Pete, please!"

"Never!"

This domestic altercation silenced the official speakers, silenced every voice but theirs – or rather Petra's. "I suppose that's what I should have expected. Mr Bloody Cautious. Don't touch me!" She made a route for herself. She grasped Len Williams by the strap of his tape recorder.

"Come on. I can do this on my own. Fact is, I'd prefer it."

Petra strode for the door. The gathering was audience to the first dramatic performance since the primary school's Christmas *Puss in Boots*, Juliet stamping out on her Romeo, the old story in tatters. Isolated in the spotlight of attention was Luke the sleepwalker. Bereft of lines to speak, he turned to stage-left. He sensed all eyes until Nigel, winning the gratitude of the embarrassed multitude, brought up the music to full power, and restored rhythm to the evening if not good spirits.

What happened? Nobody knew. "Red hair," decided Freda, "red temper."

Ron, alone, seemed to have read the situation with a degree of accuracy. "He's seen the light. Now she's on her own."

Ruth burned him to a cinder with dragon eyes. "Nice one, you little, wet fart – but you're up a gum tree as usual. We're behind her. Including you, chummy, if you know which side your bread's buttered on!"

Luke's worst shock came with the realisation that he would not be able to talk things out with Petra. Always at the back of his mind had been the comfort that, when everybody had left, when the house was still and empty, the differences between him and Petra could be swiftly resolved. He would tell her about Stacey's phone call. Though she might not agree with the position he had taken, she'd at least understand.

Yet Petra had packed her bag, tidied and hoovered the spare room, then moved out. She had joined the Siren Sisters on the barge. She was back in her old world, and for good.

His shortsightedness, coming on top of everything else, stirred in Luke a rage at himself he had never experienced before. This is the unhappiest night of your life, and just what you deserve: the cock-up king of the century.

And don't go on about having good motives. Thanks to me, Pete's more determined than ever to do the play, to stick her hand in the flames. By trying to slow her down, I've probably provoked her to be more reckless. And because I stood my ground, with that plank-head Ron giving me all the support I could do without, the Sisters will cheer her on: it's the battle of the sexes all over again.

"What on earth's the matter with you two, Luke?" Alfred stood at his son's bedroom door. Luke lay flat on his face, head stuffed in a pillow, hands thrusting the pillow against his cheeks. "Well?" Getting no response other than a grunt, Alfred sat on the bed. A hand dropped lightly on to Luke's head, smoothed the hair, as gentle as Vera's touch had been. "You think I don't understand?"

In his dreams, and in his waking hours, Luke stonewalled all questions. Connie, seated in her wheelchair above the magnificent alpine garden Luke had made for her, echoed Alfred:

"What the devil's got into you, Luke Waller?" She had stared down at him as he hacked at the vegetable plot beyond a new-sown lawn. He poured with sweat. Hard labour was his answer, his only answer at the present. Work makes one forget. He'd read it on the back of a matchbox.

"Well, young man?"

Luke had glanced up into the sun. The word in his mouth was 'Nothing', though it meant 'Everything'. He simply exhaled hot air into hot air.

"Have you seen that girl since your ridiculous quarrel?"

Alfred had said, "The house'll be like a cemetery without her." He had put his feelings into the same words when

Vera had left. He'd been right on both counts. "You looked over the precipice, son, and tried to draw her back."

Yes Dad, and ended up shoving her over.

"The day before your mother left, I walked to Mellport. I touched the stone – perhaps I should have kicked it."

Touch the stone.

"What about your own precipice, Dad – now you've decided to lead a protest march to the forest?"

"Modest in number, Luke, peaceful in intention. But we must make our mark, not let people think we don't care."

I've pushed Pete over the precipice; and Dad's decided to jump with her.

"You're dealing with killers, Dad."

Connie: "I've the patience of Job, young man. I can wait all day for an answer. Have you seen that girl?"

"No, Connie." He mumbled something else which she did not catch, and he didn't hear above the sound of his own puff. Eyes down. Heart down. All week and no sight of her.

Connie was delivering a sermon about youth, hope, love and human misunderstandings, but Luke registered nothing. All week and not a sign, not a word, except for twice-daily accounts from Alfred on how well the Siren Sisters were doing in the town; how busy they were, with street shows, busking, chorusing and folk-dancing to Amy's stirring music. "She's a degree in Electronics, you know."

"And don't think you can obliterate your troubles with rakes and spades, young man. The answer doesn't lie in the soil."

"No, Connie."

"I can tell you, the pain's worse when you stop."

"Yes, Connie." He dug, spade-flash, deep; attacking the earth, smashing the lumps, kicking the blade against

144

all resistance; muscles burning; skin burning with the sun; hands burning round the hot, slippery handle of the spade.

Alfred: "They really are polished entertainers, Luke. The heartening thing is that they're getting the locals involved – with extempore plays. There's going to be a show on Carnival afternoon, all the kids . . . You're not listening Luke."

"Yes I am, Dad."

"You're not listening, Luke."

"Yes I'm not, Connie."

"Yes you're not? What kind of gobbledegook is that?"

"Must get on, Connie. Must get on."

Yes is no – what did it matter? Since the quarrel, everything had been about-face. Luke suddenly hated his paper round, shut his eyes and mind to the rapturous sunrise. The relish for turning people's gardens into masterpieces of form and pattern and colour, faded. Stuff oxalis; stuff geraniums; stuff next spring's azaleas. I'd burn the lot, spray it with Strontium-90.

I'm no longer nice to know.

Worst of all had been the week at Monarch, doomed to closure: the sad jokes, about taking trips to the Costa del Dole, starting a whisky distillery with the redundancy money, or publishing a national newspaper which told the truth – and not one of them had extracted a smile from Luke. They should be hopping mad, not turning the other cheek.

Yes, a great example you are, Luke Waller: silent and sullen. A useless ball of spit. You go on at Dad for feeling sorry for himself. Look who's talking!

Shut up. Just shut up and dig. So he dug, turned, spread, hacked, dug, kicked, twisted and drowned his thoughts in salt. In brine – brine? Yes, for it corrodes more than metal.

Madge on Tuesday: "Go and make it up with her,

145

Luke." Ellen, with lipstick on Bill Gordon's office window: FAINT HART NEVER WON FAIR MADE. Removing the message with cleaning fluid, and not impressed by Ellen's spelling, Bill Gordon added to the chorus of persuasion: "The girls are right, Luke – you've put a blight on the place."

"After all," Freda had said with grandmotherly reassurrance, "everything's so sweet when lovers kiss and make up."

"I know you took your stand to protect Pete, Luke," Alfred had argued. "But she's got the bit between her teeth now. Nothing will stop her. What's more, the cat's creeping out of the bag."

Bit? Does he mean byte? Cat – what cat; and who put it in the bag? "Dad, are we speaking the same language?"

"Publicity, you clodpole. The news of the dumping is seeping through the community."

"Seeping? Dad, thanks to you it's flooding." Alfred did not contest the description. If the bit was in Petra's teeth it was also in the teeth of the Red Reverend: the 'living time-bomb of nuclear waste beneath our soil', as Alfred had put it in his Monday evening address to the Women's Institute, had gathered into an obsession.

The local free-sheet, *Wednesday Scene*, printed a full report and placed alongside it a rather flattering picture of Alfred, looking a little like Abraham Lincoln without the beard. The headline read:

WYNSTER'S RED REVEREND
HAMMERS NUKE DUMP PLANS

"Britain," the *Wednesday Scene* quoted Alfred as saying, "has become the nuclear dustbin of the world; and Wynster's old leadmines are, it seems, to become the first unofficial nuclear sewer."

"The damage has been done, Connie."

"Nonsense, young man. Defeatism taints your generation, if you don't mind my saying. If we stand together against these nuclear trespassers – "

"I don't mean that, Connie. The damage between us, Petra and me." It had been Luke's stock reply to Madge and Ellen and Freda and Bill Gordon, and finally to Connie.

"Luke, at your age, anything can be put right. That's what being young's all about. You can make a hash of things and you've still got time to try again."

Luke continued digging.

"Stubborn, stiff as the Mellport Stone – that's your family. On your mum's side, that is. Vera was everything but flexible." No response. "I suppose you'll want a cup of tea."

"No thanks, Connie. Must get on." Dig. Kick. Turn. Spread. Dig, Kick. Sweat. Puff. And when he got home, Luke climbed the moor. He stared down River Meadow towards *The Lucky Dragon*. He addressed the silence:

"Am I the only one in these parts who's feeling rotten?" But the silence – his old friend and standby – granted him no favours.

Chapter 8

"What the hell's up with her?" Ron to Adrienne; both staring down-stage at Petra.

"I'm sorry, I wasn't – "

"Concentrate!" hurled Ron. "We can't keep going over this – after all, it's your bloody play we're rehearsing."

"It's her body vibes," considered Luce, "they're out of orbit with Venus."

Definitely out of orbit. Colliding with things, knocking things over, missing out whole paragraphs, never mind a sentence or two: a grade-one mess. Ron's lovingly constructed forest of poles, with leaf bunches sprayed at the crown of each, and green light bulbs strung round the trunks, had suffered a slight earth tremor as Petra had crashed into them.

"Just stop wandering about. You're not even supposed to be on stage."

"I'm restless, that's all."

"You can say that again – but don't!"

Ruth emerged from a cloud of cigar smoke. "He's not worth it, Pete. None of them's worth a monkey's piss." She turned to Luce who had been practising the role of a heavy goods vehicle. "Right, Luce?"

The heavy goods vehicle mistook this for a cue to get on with the rehearsal. She switched on the ignition and with a gutteral growl accelerated across stage, shouting "Ice cream! Ice cream! Fresh ice cream . . . Made from contaminated spring water!" Which was another mess, because this was Amy's line.

"Take a breather, loves," announced Adrienne, smiling.

"We're all getting a bit overwrought."

Ron pointed at Petra: "It's her bloody depressions. They're poisoning the whole atmosphere."

Petra remained silent. She shrugged. She went and sat at the edge of the apron stage which extended over the river bank from *The Lucky Dragon.*

"Well, trouble?" Adrienne gave Petra a comforting hug. She touched her hair lightly with fingers and palm. "I've never seen you like this."

"I've never been like this ... I mean, why's he not come down? Why's he not made any attempt to –?"

"He's punishing you," Ruth had decided. "You stepped out of line. Men never forgive that. Made your own decision – that's a hanging offence. What's worse, you humiliated him in public. Which means you broke the Eleventh Commandmant – *Thou Shalt Never Hurt Male Pride.*"

Petra turned to Adrienne. "Do you think that?"

"I'd say he was just scared to death."

"Confused as a cat in a sack," came in the one male among the Sirens. "And he's better off that way. So you don't go trying to patch things up ... Come Monday, we up-sticks and head for safer waters."

"I like it here," said Amy, timid yet resolute.

"You like it everywhere." That ended Amy's contribution; but none of the Siren Sisters was ever left stranded. Luce came to Amy's aid:

"If Amy likes it, so do I. Maybe we should settle for a while. After all, the beer's out of this world. And what good can artists do if they're constantly on the move, never putting down roots?"

They all smiled, except Ron, for these words were straight from Petra's script: a speech cut from the text because it had been considered over-long.

Adrienne: "Those are your amazing true thoughts, aren't they, Pete?"

"She's mellowed," said Ruth. "A far cry from when she jumped on board that night on the Regent's Canal and refused to budge. "Take me anywhere – please! I'll cook, darn your socks, swab the deck . . . Anything if I can join you. If you let me come in through your magic mirror . . ." We almost threw you overboard, but Adrienne guessed you'd just grab the rudder and hold on till we got to Aldershot . . . Those were the days. Jesus Christ, Pete, what's happened?"

Posters had gone up all over town: the Siren Sisters invited those citizens still capable of lifting a leg above the knee to join the company in a barn dance at the Wynster's edge. Dancing to viola, concertina and moonlight would be free. There would be a collection for Africa. Home-brew, turnip turnovers and magic Eccles cakes would be on sale.

At last the *Rowmanton & Wynster Messenger* recognised both the oncoming Wynster Carnival and the presence of the Siren Sisters. Yet the message of the *Messenger* was resentful and hostile. The paper's front-page story accused the Reverend Alfred Waller of planning to turn a day of family fun into a political stunt:

WYNSTER'S CARNIVAL MARCH PUTS PROTEST BEFORE FUN

Plans to demonstrate at alleged chemical dumping in Furmiston Forest

The report attacked Alfred for 'gross manipulation of a day of pleasure for all the family'. He was using this innocent and commendable event to 'mount a sensationalised assault upon the activities of a private company earning wealth for the nation'. In its leader column, the newspaper declared:

'We say that the march should be banned forthwith. The police are equipped with powers to do so – otherwise the public peace, not to mention public and private property, will be at risk.

It is high time the so-called "Red Reverend" went back to preaching simple Christian virtues rather than tampering in issues which are none of his concern.

We say: the business of the Church is prayer. Leave business to the businessmen and politics to the politicians.

In three little words: BELT UP ALF!'

Councillor Hartfield had been on Alfred's doorstep almost before the newspaper's ink was dry. "Call off the Carnival, Noel?"

"Not the Carnival, Reverend – the March."

"But we've people coming from all over the country."

"To march on Furmiston?"

"No. To parade through the town."

"Whatever for?"

"We all agreed . . . A celebration, of goodwill and unity."

Councillor Hartfield waved the *Messenger* in the air as if he were swatting mosquitoes of the Militant Tendency. "It's become political, Reverend – political!"

At Sir No-all's insistence, an emergency meeting of the Carnival Committee was summoned for Friday evening. He had been unmoved when reminded that Friday was supposed to be reserved for all those in Wynster Bridge, including the Carnival Committee, who wished to raise a leg above the knee. "Let the goddamn barn dance wait!"

"Len, there's a young man on the phone – Luke Waller."

Put him on . . . Luke?"

"Mr Williams, if you want that interview, I've changed my mind."

"How come?"

"I was trying to protect my dad's Carnival from being the cause of the next world war. After all, it was supposed to be for Peace and Pleasure. Now everybody's gunning for it, I can't just stand by and say nothing."

"Right, will you be at tonight's Emergency Meeting?"

"Yes."

"That's when you should speak up."

"To them?"

"Think about it. It'll be better than coming from your dad all the time: the voice of youth for once. I'll record it."

"I can't make a speech, not in front of everybody."

"Practise . . . Your friend Pete dried up, by the way. She's another audience you ought to be practising a speech for."

Alfred checked his delight at Luke's hesitant offer to address the Emergency Meeting. "This isn't going to be about the lifestyle of the British badger, you know. Noel's got a head of steam and there are plenty backing him."

"You think I'll blow it, don't you?"

Father had grabbed son's wrist. He lifted it up. "Look, you're shaking already."

"Well, thank the Lord I don't talk through my left wrist."

"Fair enough." Alfred was surprised, wary and doubtful, but he gripped the hand that shook. He held it firm. "Okay, Mr Orator-Come-Lately, you're booked. Now . . . this is what I think you ought to say."

"Dad, the last thing people'll want while there's a barn dance going to waste, is one of your sermons."

"I can still give you an old trouper's advice. So, make that first sentence count."

"Yes, Dad."

"Avoid too many adjectives."

"Yes, Dad."

"Be concrete, factual and stay with examples that are part of your audience's experience."

"Audience? It'll just be the Committee, won't it?"

"Heavens, no. The whole town will be there."

Luke's spirits slumped. "Why did I open my big mouth?"

"That's right – open it wide and project your voice to the back of the hall. What's most important, maintain a firm eye-contact, don't go staring up at the rafters."

"You do, Dad. You spend most of your sermons with your eyes on Judas in the West window."

"That, idiot, is because I expect him to walk off with the silver . . . Just do what I say, son, not what I do. Oh, and one last thing – in debate, always try to anticipate the arguments of the opposition."

"Better than the pub, Don."

"Only when it's shut."

The hunters spread through the scorching afternoon; a private army let loose on nature with shot-guns, air-rifles, even crossbows. Everything that flies, everything that panics amid the silent green glades, shoot: execute the forest.

"Go fetch!" Dogs followed the cartridge. Dogs brought back the victims, bloodied with shot, bolt-shattered. "Go fetch!" Partridge, wood pigeon, stoat, rabbit.

"Like the good old days, Don."

"They're coming again."

"Angola?"

"Home ground, Sandy."

Grey squirrel, pigeon, crow, jay. "What we're protecting is so bloody dangerous, it'll make security the biggest service industry in the country. Go fetch!" Pheasant, skylark, hare, barn owl. "But Furmiston's the pioneer. A test case. Business has got to be convinced it works. Up there's the future. And wherever they stick the stuff - that's our future."

"Scares the shit out of me, Don, to be honest."

"Me too, but how else would we make this kind of money?"

"Robbing banks, wheeling and dealing on the Stock Exchange . . ."

"Amounts to the same thing . . . Go fetch!"

"What about Stacey, Don?"

"She should never have read that kid's diary. Discovered a conscience as big as Aussieland, and as bloody useless. But Down Under's where she'll be if she talks."

"And them kids, Don?"

"Kids? I shouldn't have used the word. With luck on their side, they could scupper the whole enterprise. They've got the vision of the innocent, the sort who spotted the trick with the Emperor's New Clothes. The adults round these parts don't worry me – but that redhead and her squire, they're the enemy . . . Good shooting, Luigi."

"Grazie, Don. I shoot the commies better."

"You do that."

"How many will be joining us for the big day, Don?"

"A coach load . . . real patriots."

"I'll bet."

"Vero. Two my Belgian friends, they want un piccolo piece of the action."

Ahead, the dogs barked with the relish of discovery. Along the rise where the bank soared among oaks, dogs sniffed, tails beat. "What is it, Shad?" In their frenetic eagerness, the dogs were fighting each other to squeeze into the badger sett. "What've you found, eh? Go fetch!"

The wastepaper bin overflowed, and still Luke had not managed to include any of Alfred's advice in his speech. In truth, "Ladies and gentlemen, unaccustomed as I am . . ." was as far as he had got. He had, however, listed possible arguments of the opposition:

THE MARCH WILL
—make the town untidy and thus land the ratepayer with unnecessary cleaning bills;
—offend the people who have purchased Furmiston and dissuade them from bringing much-needed jobs to the area;
—cause more bother than it's worth (i.e. whoever heard of a protest march achieving anything)?

THEREFORE IT IS ONLY COMMON SENSE TO
—forget all about the dumping because it will go on whether we like it or not;
—trust that the dumping is in safe hands and that those responsible know what they are doing, otherwise those in authority would not let them do it;
—enjoy the present because 'it may never happen'.

TO IGNORE THE ABOVE ARGUMENTS WOULD BE TO
—play into the hands of radicals and other trouble-makers;
—set a bad example to people in other parts of the country faced with similar unavoidable hazards;
—obscure the real issues pressing upon the district, namely the closure of Monarch Paints, the dispute at Ecclestone's and the dangerous state of the town's roads, pavements, sewers and street lighting (not to mention the church steeple which is getting to look like the Leaning Tower of Pisa).

The only point worth a candle, Luke thought, is the one about Monarch and Ecclestone's. Yet who's busting a gut to save Monarch, or support the women?

Which leaves me with what?

He glanced down at his notes on the dangers to the population of leaks of nuclear waste: a sorry case of, 'So what?' – till it happens, that is. Till folks can actually feel their bones rotting with cancer, their lungs punctured, their bodies leaking blood internally . . . Till then, it's like the dangers of smoking. Death happens to other people. It's unreal.

After all, release radiation into the air and what do you see? Nowt. It simply spreads invisibly on the wind. It settles, sinks into the soil. Grass grows. Cows eat it. Humans drink their milk . . . Like a fairy story? As frightening as a panto villain.

Funny thing: it doesn't matter how many brains you've got if you can't draw a picture in your head. Without imagination, you're finished. On the march will be people who've got imagination – that's their value; who've seen what's in the air: in their heads. And it's a gift they must communicate to others.

From the opposition's point of view, then, that's why the event should be banned, because marches are a way of making the blind see. Luke was impressed by Dad's advice; even more at Alfred's stubbornness in holding out for the march. He's not all piss and wind.

Alfred stopped counting those entering Church Hall for the emergency meeting once he had reached a hundred and fifty. Poor Luke. He had expected to address fifteen at most. At least some things stir people up, bring them out from behind their tellies, though in this instance I'm not sure what's done the stirring; or whether they're here to sing praises or string me up by my ankles.

Hiding his doubts behind a broad and inane grin, Alfred scanned the faces. Perhaps it was the story in one of this morning's national tabloids which had attracted them:

ALFRED THE RED SETS CAT AMONG TOWN PIGEONS

Naturally the paper got most of its facts wrong: the Red Reverend had at no time been protesting against the siting of an American army signalling station; at no time had he 'savaged US foreign policy in Central America'; well, at least not recently. The paper quoted Councillor Hartfield as predicting 'utter chaos in the streets of Wynster Bridge, if the Lefties get their parade'.

"I never said 'Lefties'." Noel had privately apologised to Alfred. "Fact is, I never spoke to the paper at all, though I admit it's probably what I might have said." He was relieved to hear that this, in Alfred's eyes, made a whole lot of difference.

If I knew how to faint, thought Luke as he saw the audience bulge and keep on bulging, I'd faint. He'd once had to give a short talk to his class. It had been a disaster. The stutter he acquired in those moments took weeks to shake off; and so did the coughing fit caused by the fluids in his mouth deserting via his tonsils. Or something like that.

At least there was no sign of the Siren Sisters, busy preparing the barn dance down by the river. And no Pete to wither him with a glance.

When Councillor Hartfield stood up to speak, Luke had the doubtful privilege of having anticipated practically every word: "Marches, ladies and gentlemen, have their place – and Wynster Bridge is not their place. For marches occur when there's something wrong – and there's nothing the matter with Wynster which cannot be handled in the proper way, with common sense and through official channels."

Luke was so thunderously nervous he caught only fragments of the Councillor's speech: 'desperately important to bring jobs to the area . . . science has solved the problem of nuclear waste . . . proper safeguards have made dumping as safe as your back garden . . . dangers have been grossly exaggerated . . . and what about cigarette smoking . . ? we had cancer long before there was nuclear power . . . if we don't reap the financial gains, somebody else will . . . trying to make political capital, embarrass the authorities . . . not certain what the firm is, but I'm confident . . . a lot of unwelcome strangers trampling over . . . litter everywhere . . . bricks through shop windows . . . permitting CND banners. Friends of the Earth placards, Greenpeace whales . . . playing into the hands of radicals and other trouble-makers . . . this town has been an example . . . returning the same Member of Parliament for twenty-five . . . obscure the real problems facing . . . the closure of Monarch, the dispute at . . . the state of the drains . . . in short – '

Connie Hillsmore had manoeuvred herself into a prominent position at the front of the audience. "Time to give somebody else a say, Noel!"

The Councillor still had at least three more sheets of A4 to get through, and had no intention of giving way until Madge, shrill and direct as ever, called him a musty old sheep. "We want that parade, Councillor. Our Deborah has spent weeks doin' her costume and our Craig has put more hours into that Carnival float than you've had hot dinners."

Alfred was encouraged. There was plenty of support for Madge's point of view. He joined Noel on the stage.

Luke was close, staring not into the rafters but at his feet. "Friends," said Alfred, "you know my position. I want the Carnival to go on as planned – and that includes our parade through the town . . . But I want something more. I want us to be clear about the issue that's in all our minds, and which Councillor Hartfield has touched upon."

He paused. He signalled Luke to come up. "And that issue, in a very real sense, involves everyone, especially our young people . . . Who listens to what they have to say these days?"

"Nobody!" responded Madge. "The Government don't care a bugger!"

"No politics, madam!" snapped Councillor Hartfield.

"It's all politics!"

Alfred soothed the combatants and then continued:

"Ladies and gentlemen, I'm going to ask Luke here to have his say. He has his own views and, well – over to you, Luke."

There was a ripple of applause as Luke stepped forward. He'd written something out on a postcard, but the hand that held the card seemed as if it was at the bottom of a mountain while he was at the top. Cards don't shake like aspen leaves in the wind, so it must be the hand that was shaking.

He took ten seconds shuffling his feet, even though all that was necessary was for them to point in the same direction. The audience was patient, tolerant, but any time now they would also be shuffling their feet.

"Luke?" A gentle reminder that the speech was due for delivery tonight, not next week. "It's all yours."

A phrase came to him: you are waterlogged with terror. He stared at the ocean of faces; people he had known all his life, if only by sight. He began, inaudibly: "At first, I . . ." Alfred's rules about speech-making were about to go down like skittles: grab them with the first sentence; protect your voice; maintain eye-contact.

"Speak up, young man!" commanded Connie.

"Spit it out, son!" advised Freda.

"At first, ladies and gentlemen . . ."

"That's better."

"At first, I began to agree . . . with Councillor Hartfield." He sensed the inner groan among his friends. That's right, Luke, shoot yourself in the foot. "At first, that is. Because I panicked . . ."

"Anybody can panic, Luke," reassured Madge. "Don't blame yourself."

"That's what I've done ever since – blamed myself, for being an ostrich." He halted, completely out of breath. "For letting everybody down."

Everybody? Where was Pete to hear this public confession? For 'everybody', read 'somebody'.

"We don't feel let down one bit, Luke. We all loves you!" Ellen stirred a modest cheer and gave Luke time to draw in air, and to relive the most painful moment of his life. "Sod off! Mr Bloody Cautious. Don't touch me!" Pete's last words. I'll remember that look till the day I die.

Alfred, in a whisper: "Get on with it, son."

The panic was creeping back. Luke's mind had become a void again. He stared at the audience. On the point of capitulation into total silence, he relived another snapshot of his past:

"Stop it there, son!" Torchlight in the face. "You looking for something?"

"Just walking."

"We're wondering just where you're walking, son."

His first dismissal from the moors; Luke's land. "Ladies and gentlemen, I've lived in these parts all my life." He was like an old wind-up gramophone being jerked into action

160

with a desperate clanking of the handle. "All my life – and I love it: the hills, the woods, the glens, the streams. And its inhabitants. Everything!"

"Good on ye, Luke – you tell 'em!"

"Thanks, Madge. Well, until a few weeks ago, all that was free. You could walk where you liked. But this I can tell you, from personal experience – it's not free any longer."

"Shame!"

"Yes, a shame. Whatever those people are doing up there, one thing's clear: you're not allowed. Try it for yourselves. You'll get torches shone in your faces. They'll tell you to keep to the road, don't stray – go home. I mean, does it matter how dangerous the stuff is that they're dumping, if suddenly people aren't allowed anywhere near? If they're not allowed to walk their own hills?"

"Hell, no!" burst out Bill Gordon.

"I've been there. With my friend Pete. It's not us who've dreamed up those twelve foot high fences, the razor wire, the guard dogs. We've not invented blokes with rifles. If you don't believe us – we've photographs to prove it. Or Pete has."

"Good for Pete!"

"Anybody who asks questions, they follow. I've been followed. They watch you. They treat you as if you'd actually stolen their precious waste. Once you're in their sights, they never let you alone."

He hesitated, yet free of nerves now, without a blank mind. Indeed his mind was teeming with words. "That might be good for business, but it's no good for freedom." He let the thought sink in. He sensed in himself a strange power.

"I want to ask you: what rights have we got if we can't wander in our own countryside? It's not just their fence they are protecting. It's the approaches to the fence.

161

And then they want to stop us talking about their fence, asking questions about it."

He waited. He knew, for the present at least, the argument was won. "People want us to cancel the parade, to back down. That's what they want up in Furmiston. If we do what they want, that won't be the end of it. Of backing down. It won't be enough for them. That's my view."

Now he threw his voice to the back of the hall; now he maintained eye-contact. "Soon, the only free place in this country will be inside your head!"

The roar of applause which greeted the end of Luke's speech persuaded Councillor Hartfield not to insist on a right of reply. "Be it on your own heads," is all he would say.

Connie Hillsmore seized on the moment: "All those in favour of proceeding with the march as planned – say aye!" The forest of hands and ayes was denser than Furmiston. "Okay, the ayes have it. Now let's get to that barn dance before they pack up for want of support!"

"My dear Charles, this is Great Britain, not South Africa. We can't shut down newspapers because they print embarrassing information. Naturally every Government ministry would prefer a total blackout of information, but there can be no guarantees."

Charles Rhodes of Disposal Services International, subsidiary of Star Oil, stared at his dinner guest in the restaurant of his London club. "I've had reporters on the phone to me all day. They're wreckers and this company, having invested over five million, is taking no chances."

"Charles, you're fretting needlessly. Let them clamour. Let them stir up the community with their sensational headlines. The population will become marginally interested, then downright bored."

162

"In the meantime, what are we supposed to do?"

"Sit tight. Deny everything – well, almost everything. In a month the issue of nuclear dumping will be cold potatoes. How long did Chernobyl stay in the news? Till Wimbledon, if that. There's nothing so safe as yesterday's news. Before the summer's over, there'll be an inner city riot or the announcement of a royal baby. Profits will flow as usual."

Rhodes smiled, though not amused. "Some democracy you've got here."

"It works, Charles."

This time Rhodes leaned across the table. "Very well, we'll sweat out the headlines for the present . . . But my board of directors want that march in Wynster Bridge banned. On that, we intend to sit tight."

Luke stood in front of his bedroom mirror. "Now who's going for glory?" After the excitement of a speech which had amazed Luke about himself, as well as surprised all those who knew him as Mr Stutter, he was hit by doubts.

Mirror, mirror on the wall, who's the fire-raiser of them all?

After giving due credit to his son for 'a speech that did honour to the name of Civil Liberties', Alfred had reverted to practicalities: "Two things, Luke. Stay in for your mother's call and – are you listening, or still reliving your triumph?"

Impatiently: "Two things, Dad, and you've told me them ten times. Wait for Vera's call and be a good boy. Go to the barn dance."

They had known since teatime of Alfred's summons to meet his church superior for 'a little chat'. "I'm in trouble, son. Alfred the Muck Stirrer is back up to his axles again."

"What'll they do to you this time, Dad, burn you at the stake?"

163

"The Catholics do that, son. We simply get a tap on the wrist with a damp ecclesiastical towel."

Jacket potatoes would have stayed hot in the stifling air. Heat rose, full of smells from surfaces baked by the day's tireless sun. The world's crying out to be hosed down. Nervous, restless, far more troubled inside than he could explain, Luke listened to the sounds of the barn dance drifting up the valley.

He talked to the wardrobe: "Anything special for a knees-up?" You've not much option, came the reply: there's what you're wearing and these black cords. Always too stiff. He tried them: as planks; I can hardly bend them, never mind lift a knee.

If I get dressed up, she'll think I'm . . .

The phone rang. He hurtled downstairs. "Yes, Luke Waller – Vera!" Eight forty-five exactly: dead on time.

"Luke, I'm sorry. I'm going to have to disappoint you both. I can't make it tomorrow."

His grin broke like a cup on the kitchen floor. In every mental picture Luke had of the Carnival, Vera was present, in centre view. "That's terrible. Dad's banked everything on your coming."

"Then more fool him! I said 'maybe' this weekend – "

"Carnival weekend!"

"Carnivals are not top of my agenda at the moment, Luke. There's something on down here."

"There's something on up here – and not just the Carnival."

"Don't shout, Luke. You must get used to the way things are and not how you'd wish them to be. And then explain to your father. Something's come up. I can't explain on the phone."

"Vera, this has all been done for your sake . . . all this!"

"Neither of you understands a thing, do you? I've my life. You've yours. They're separate now."

"At least phone again . . . put it gently to him."

"You can do that, Luke. I'm sorry. I'll try to get up later."

"It's always later."

"How's Pete and the gang?"

"Okay, I guess."

"Are you looking after her?"

He grunted: half a no, half a yes. "I've got to go, Vera – to this barn dance." The phone pips went. Neither had time or inclination at this moment to add anything more meaningful to the exchange. Not even goodbye.

He was in the act of replacing the phone on the hook, when he dropped it in shock. He ducked, covered his face with his arm, though it was too late to escape the shower of glass that enveloped him. The kitchen window had shattered. The pieces hit the sink, the floor, the kitchen table, and a brick went spinning across the stone floor.

"Luke Waller?"

He rammed his back against the wall, pulling the kitchen curtain across him. In terror, he glanced at the door – shut but not properly latched.

"Luke Waller? We've got one of your friends out here." Voice unrecognised. Not a shout, yet penetrating to the nerve. "Put up a fight. But lost."

Then silence.

"Take a look at that!" The Sisters had watched Petra step from the cabin of *The Lucky Dragon*. "The golden butterfly emerges from her chrysalis." Adrienne bowed, Luce curtsied.

"She's actually got legs!" exclaimed Ruth.

Petra tried to dodge the spotlight trained on her by Ron, but it was either the spotlight or the river so she acknowledged the scatter of applause from the barn dancers. Her dress of forest green and striped autumn gold shimmered in the light. "It's Lena's, my sister's . . ."

She shrugged, suddenly disconcerted by all this attention. "So as I had it, I thought – why not?" She permitted Adrienne, like Prince Charming, to escort her off the galleon.

"Indeed, why not?"

All eyes, all smiles. "What the hell's up with everybody?"

"We're just dazzled . . . Yesterday, Grease Monkey Pete, astride her two-wheel macho-mobile, tonight?"

"May I have the first dance, miss?" Nigel Fowles, four feet eight in his stockinged feet, five foot in his Party Specials, stepped forward right on to Petra's toe, trapped in elegantly pointed green high-heels.

Amy struck up music once more. The air danced, the night danced, to the bold notes of her viola. Ruth's concertina lifted knees and hearts, and soon the sorcery of the music lured dozens of people from homes nearby to join the hundred or so already twirling and leaping and leg lifting in Ron's yellow circle of light.

Petra could not help it, but she danced with her eyes over everybody's shoulder, her gaze wandering up River Meadow towards the town, towards the church steeple and the home of Mr Sulk. Expectant, always looking; attention for ever divided.

Bugger!

After Nigel, Freda's two eldest boys, Tim, on leave from Northern Ireland, Gerald, on leave from the Fisherman's Rest. Then the willowy Indian boy, Gihan, from the emporium on Market Square, followed by Bill Gordon, gallant and sweating drops off the end of his nose.

Even Councillor Hartfield, transformed by Ruth's special-strength hot punch from prating parrot to springheeled nanny goat, staked his claim. He whirled Petra off her feet and practically at the horizontal, letting off Highland whoops into the night.

Best-looking partner was Stan Westall, player-manager of Wynster Athletic, rattling Petra's ankles like he did the opposition on Saturday afternoons.

The people rode the roundabouts of the music. The dancing became a wild expression of the spirit; joyful, soaring – why've we never done this before? This was more than a dance, more even than a celebration; and the white wizards of The Siren Sisters Company knew this.

Petra alone resisted the entwining magic of the music and the motion and the whispering winds from the riverbank. The wizards did their best – Adrienne dancing with her, as soft as pillows; Luce, the grizzly bear with paws of gold, both incanting spells in the clammy air.

No, I cannot. I am not here. Heart-cleft. Leave me.

When Ruth announced the *Skaters' Waltz* 'for the silver-haired oldies', Petra faded from the circle of light, answering a fainter incantation but a stronger spell. Something's wrong. All evening, two minds – anger and resentment concealing deeper instincts, casting a fog over the real shape of things; yet most of all blinded by hurt pride.

"Sod it!" She ran, not caring who saw her, up the meadow, sunbaked, moonbathed, patiently awaiting the tramp of hundreds of feet tomorrow; up past the witch-eyed hawthorn, and all the way swearing out loud – at the refusal of her high heels to perform like trainers, at the dress which caught on sprays of thistle.

"You'd better have a damned good explanation, Luke Waller – so help me!"

She puffed over the ridge, traced the uneven slope to the stile in the dry-stone wall. She crashed through the wooden gate that divided moorland from garden.

"Luke?"

He was below her, deep in the darkness, still as the air, holding something; cradling it. He lifted his head.

She ran across the high lawn, down between vegetables and flowers. She stopped. there was the faintest smudge of silver light like a veil on his upper face, and the eyes were wells of tears.

"Luke – what's happened?"

He spoke with his arms. He lifted the dead badger towards her. "All of them . . . They killed all of them!"

Chapter 9

"I'm sorry, Reverend, but those are the Chief Constable's instructions: no parade through Wynster Bridge. No march to Furmiston, except for a deputation of not more than six persons."

"Why?"

"Orders of the Chief Constable."

"I didn't ask who – I asked why."

"That's all I can tell you, sir."

Alfred glared at the phone as if it were part of a plot to confound him with this appalling news. "Look, Inspector, how am I to inform the hundreds of people who are coming to tomorrow's – correction – today's Carnival?" The time was two minutes after one a.m.

"We shall have road patrols at all access points to the town, and those arriving will be properly informed of the cancellation of the parade."

"I can't believe it."

"Chief Constable's orders, sir."

"He gave us permission," came back Alfred forcefully. "Everything has been arranged – months of planning!"

"Not for the way things have turned out, Mr Waller. A quiet little town carnival and parade, yes. But now we have reason to believe there may be trouble."

"You're protecting the dumpers, then?"

"I know nothing about that, sir."

In his head, Alfred slammed the phone down: "Puppets of the Establishment!" In reality he replaced the receiver with the care of an explosives expert handling gelignite. Here we go – the ranks are closing fast.

The Reverend Alfred Waller looked up at God and sighed. "I'm wondering which side you're taking in this business . . ."

From eight thirty on Carnival morning, Petra and Luke toured the town and all roads leading to Wynster; Luke steering the Navigator, Petra using a loudhailer to broadcast the bad news:

"By order of the police, the Carnival parade through Wynster Bridge is cancelled – please make your way on foot to River Meadow . . . Carnival opens at midday prompt!"

On passing the Wynster police station, Petra had been unable to resist announcing, "Get your passes for the Berlin Wall!"

Hired lorries, piled with Carnival tableaux had to be abandoned; dragons dissolved; magic caverns collapsed. The work of weeks came down in minutes. "Please don't despair . . . Keep your costumes, bring what you can carry. Assemble at River Meadow, midday onwards."

Under the watchful eyes of police patrols, flags got furled, banners rolled up, placards lowered. "We have not been invaded from outer space," pronounced Petra, diverging more and more from the script laid down by Alfred, "just by coppers from all points of the compass . . . They're here for our protection folks."

On the country roads, the amicable disorder of the town was replicated: buses from all over had halted beyond Town Moor. "Leave your vehicle at this point," was the police command, "and proceed to town on foot."

Out stepped the Caribbean steel band from Birmingham, the Highland dancers from Rotherham, majorettes from Ashby-de-la-Zouche; contingents of CND from Kettering, Kidderminster and Cleethropes; Greenpeacers from Hull, Huntingdon and Hunstanton; Friends of the Earth from

Sheffield, Sunderland and . . . Bridgend. Out rattled bus-loads of skeletons, nuns wearing death-masks, slaves in paperchains, all being herded into straggling lines along the side of the road.

"Leave the placards – no banners . . . No parade. Proceed to River Meadow."

Also prominent among the would-be marchers were anti-dumping veterans from the officially earmarked sites for nuclear waste burial – from Fulbeck in Lincolnshire, Killingholme on Humberside, Elstow in Bedfordshire and Bradwell in Essex:

"Where's the dump?"

"Which way to the dump?"

"River Meadow is your permitted destination. No flags, Keep in single file."

Worried questioner in bare feet, soaking up melted tar: "Is there a shortcut?"

"Only if you're a crow."

Petra and Luke were up a cart track along Town Moor. Announcements continued: "The Wynster Carnival Committee apologise to all our friends . . . The parade has been cancelled on the orders of the police . . . Please bear with us."

"Where's the dump?"

"Which way to the dump?"

"Proceed to River Meadow," competed the police loudhailer.

"Furmiston Forest," countered Petra, "is out of bounds to protestors. We are sorry. Furmiston is now a no-go area . . . but please make for River Meadow. The Carnival will continue there as planned . . . And don't forget tonight's play by the Siren Sisters Company – the living newspaper that will reveal all."

"Get that redhead!" But Luke had already moved off. "I'm going to keep you so busy," Petra had said, "you'll not have a second to brood over the badgers." "But all of them!" "So they took all of them. Better than one left without parents."

Through an open gate, across a dipping field ready for winter wheat, on to a cinder track, through Barton's lower paddock and back on to the road.

They slowly followed the non-parade. Behind the steel band wound a centipede of legs under a gigantic model of a whale. Then shone the majorettes' scarlet bows on sky-blue shoes contrasting with the bare sandalled feet beneath saffron robes of the Hari Krishna priests, scalps shaved, humming in time with their leader's solemn tabor. They glanced neither to the left – at the scores of police – nor to the right, at the first amazed citizens of Wynster Bridge.

"Break it up – no marching!" It was an impossible instruction. "In tens only . . . You, stop! You, go ahead." One lot rammed another. "Okay, forget it. Just assemble on River Meadow." And out of earshot, "Jesus Christ, who's idea was this?"

Luke turned off the main road, slipped through Riley Row, over the cobbles between Mill Gap and the Old School, round by Lynwood to the town centre. All the while, Petra repeated her message.

"Come to our play on River Meadow tonight, where the facts about Furmiston will be told in full. Learn how your countryside has become out of bounds . . . Join in the debate – should big business be tipping nuclear waste into Wynster's old leadmines . . ? If you don't believe us, come tonight, and see the evidence with your own eyes."

"Pete, we're making enemies."

"They started it."

"We could end up like the badgers."

Up Mount Pleasant, along Shireoaks, across to Lower Chapel, skirting the playing fields, swinging down to

Tocholes Road where the river curled back round the town, and always just a street ahead of police cars who were now under express orders to 'grab the bitch with the blabber-mouth'.

In the town centre again, Petra's message boomed out once more, but its source baffled the police, all of them bussed in from the city. "It's got to be from one of those roofs."

"Or from above the shops."

"Nuclear waste," continued the unseen but much-heard Petra, "is the most dangerous substance on earth, ladies and gentlemen – and they're burying it in your woods ... If you take a look at any geological map of the area, you will see how the underground streams flow beneath Wynster Bridge.

"Remember, a grain of plutonium smaller than a pinch of snuff could kill the entire population of this town ... There is no such thing as harmless nuclear waste. If it enters the blood, there is the acute danger of leukaemia or lymphatic cancer, especially among children.

"Radiation causes deformity in babies and over generations could produce a race of monsters. It is your choice ... And you are making it on behalf of your children, and your children's children."

Earlier, Luke had said, "The Central Electricity Generating Board claims we're more at risk from garden fertilizer than nuclear waste."

"And do you believe one word they say?"

"I will do – "

"Oh?"

"When they start building a twelve foot fence round our back garden."

In the old bell tower adjoining the Wesleyan chapel converted to a do-it-yourself store, Petra tucked the loudhailer under her arm. "I bet you've brought a few girls up here in your time, Luke."

He shrugged. "You're the first who insisted on bringing a loudhailer.

"What did the others do to escape – jump?"

River Meadow, mid-afternoon. The West Indian steel band had given way to the pipers and dancers from the Scottish Highlands of West Yorkshire. All morning there had been activities for children, the most popular being the Siren Sisters' extempore plays performed along the river bank.

Already the result of the Battle of Hastings had been reversed: the Conqueror had been defeated by Good King Harold who distributed ice lollies to friends and foes alike, and gave the nation a 363 day holiday every year, 364 each Leap Year.

There had been races, a dance tournament, an ugly knees competition, tortoise speed trials, trips in a balloon (until the balloon lost height, landed midstream and then drifted down the afternoon with its happy cargo still on board).

Substituting for Vera, Luke Waller had become Gipsy Rose Waller, Fortune Teller to Royalty etc. He had set up shop in a blue and orange frame-tent, offering crystal ball readings at twenty pence. Palms cost twenty-five and tarot cards thirty.

There had been half an hour of speeches, a prize-giving for international yodellers, a sheepdog demonstration when two of the sheep sought refuge in Luke's tent, a motorcyle display team, an hour of Heavy Metal by a Rowmanton group called the Troglobites, a tug-of-peace, and an exhibition of falconry.

The only smidgen of cloud in a peerless sky came with the fancy dress competition when Noel Hartfield was booed by a pacifist contingent for selecting an entrant clad as a British grenadier. However, Connie Hillsmore restored equilibrium by choosing for the second prize a child representing a white dove of peace.

"Cosy in here." Petra thrust her palm under the nose of Gypsy Rose Waller.

"Twenty-five pence for palms, madam."

"I'll owe you." She stretched out her hand between both of his.

"Honest, I've not an inkling what I'm supposed to look for."

"Don't kid me, Gypsy. A long and happy life, that's what you're supposed to be reading. The lifeline – it's there somewhere."

He examined her hand. "Vera knows . . . She used to have queues outside the tent." He turned her hand over. "It's sacrilege to bite the nails of such beautiful hands."

"Come on, stop stalling. What does the palm tell you?"

"Close your eyes, then." Luke fished under his Gypsy Rose dress into his trouser pocket. He had worried that the right moment might never arrive. He folded Petra's fingers over a pair of earrings, bought with his last pay from Monarch, and an offer to wash and vacuum the jeweller's car. "Instructions from the crystal ball."

She opened her eyes. She turned the earrings in her hand. "Do you know, my dad did the same when he gave me the keys of the Norton." She cocked her head, deeply touched. "You're beautiful, Luke."

Behind the gypsy veil, one flushed face. "They're blue john. Special kind of fluorspar . . . They'll bring you luck."

"Does the palm say I'll be needing it?" She did not press him for an answer. "I like them. Very much." She removed her own, single earring, partner to the one lost outside the police van at the Peace Camp.

"Here." She gave it to him. "Till I can get you something."

At the entrance to the frame-tent, Petra looked around. "You know what? This rig is just what we need. We could pitch it at the entrance to Furmiston. Make our protest like the Peace Campers . . . Start the ball rolling."

"Together?"

"Strictly no sexism."

"It'd be too hot for a tent."

"And when the snow came?"

Luke took his chance: to hope. "In these parts, when the snow falls – there's no more wonderful place on earth."

She smiled. "We'd need a double sleeping bag . . ."

Early evening, and a delegation of six persons was all the police would permit to lodge a protest at the gates of Furmiston Forest; and for a period of fifteen minutes only. "It's a stupid regulation, Inspector," asserted Petra.

Alfred Waller agreed. He surveyed the once-lonely forest. "I mean, why so many police?"

"We're here to maintain the peace, Reverend."

"I hadn't realised peace was under threat."

"Peace has nothing to do with it," said Petra. "You're here to shield a multi-national company that's been caught with its pants down."

"Listen, young – "

"Are you investigating the legality of what these people are doing? Answer me that!"

"I'll answer you nothing. And any more lip from you, and we'll have your arse out of here."

Luke calmed Petra. "If you get yourself arrested, what'll happen to the play?"

She nodded, but her anger simmered. "It's just not right . . . You're a protection racket!"

Councillor Hartfield had insisted on being a member of the delegation, to counterbalance the presence of a representative of CND, and to keep an eye on Connie. To give him his due, Sir No-all had wheeled her the last three-quarters of a mile of forest track, for the police had not permitted any vehicles to approach.

To Luke's surprise, Noel showed a mood more akin to Petra's than might have been predicted: "It seems rather a waste of ratepayers' money, Inspector, to have three police cars and at least fifteen officers to guard one country gate."

"No further, please."

"We'd like to talk to the guard," said John, the CND man from Barrow-in-Furness. "At least put our case to somebody."

"I'm sorry – "

"Sorry?"

"Orders. You can address anyone in front of the fence, but not behind it."

Noel Hartfield: "Young man, this is a free country. Talking to a person is not a crime, surely, and ought not to require permission in triplicate. We want to know exactly what is going on in our neck of the woods."

Connie beamed and clapped her hands. "At last – my hero!"

Don Neeson's Toyota Landcruiser returned to camp along the straight forest track. He was accompanied by Luigi.

Alfred celebrated. "Now we can talk!"

"Keep clear!" The protestors were brushed to the side of the track, allowing the Landcruiser to stop with its bonnet almost touching the gate. The guard was out, unlocking. Don and Luigi looked ahead of them. Two more sentries had emerged from the guard hut, neither of them armed except for short truncheons worn at the belt.

Petra broke from her police escort. She banged on the side of the Toyota with her fist. "We want to talk, Don

Neeson!" She was grabbed, dragged back. "You said we could talk . . ."

Don had had his window wide open. He rolled it up, still staring fixedly to the front.

"They're mercenaries: they'll terrorise everybody that gets in their way – yet who's protecting them?"

"You said we could talk, Officer," reminded Noel.

There was no response. The gates were open. Petra wrenched free and made a dash for the gap between Landcruiser and fence. She was caught, hurled across the track and almost disappeared down a bank of ferns.

Nobody had been watching Luke. He was aboard the Landcruiser as it shot forward, clutching on to its tail, one foot lodged on the towing bar. He was through the gates, only for the police to give chase and the men from the guard hut to go for him with fists and feet.

"They're murderers!" he heard himself cry as he folded under blows. The police did not give the guards time to really get to work. Still shouting about the murder of the badgers, 'and half the wildlife of this forest', Luke was ejected down the same bank of ferns which had welcomed Petra.

"I'm okay." He stood. He'd suffered nettles again. Everyone was confused, outraged, distraught – except Petra.

"Round one to us," she called.

The performance of the never-to-be-forgotten, never-to-be-repeated epic, *Poison Pie; Or – If You Go Down in the Woods Tonight . . . You're sure of a Nasty Surprise*, was only moments away. It was dark. The moon had been showing for ages, another performer awaiting an audience of stars.

Luke surveyed River Meadow. "A perfect auditorium," Adrienne had said; and it was now concealed beneath a bumper crop of spectators. He had sold over a hundred programmes. Alfred, across the twilit rows of faces of all ages, locals from Wynster Bridge and Rowmanton, and many who had taken part in the Carnival, had run out of programmes altogether.

Earlier, there had been a nervous, stand-up tea with the players; all on edge, including Petra who could not keep still and repeatedly offered Adrienne the chance to sack her as narrator: "I just sound terrible."

"You're fine. Clear as a bell and full of feeling."

"And what if I lose my balance in that thing? I've no head for heights."

At this comment, Ron's chest puffed out and his eyebrows pushed furrows into his hairline. "That tower is as tough as the Severn Bridge, lady. And if you fall out, it's because you're a chronic fidget."

Petra's next fear was about the play. "It's a stupid script. I should have made it more . . . nasty."

"And lose your audience's goodwill? Nonsense. It'll do. It gets its point over."

"But what *is* the point?"

"Luke," begged Ron, "go and drown this ratbag, will you?"

Refusing to give ground, the ratbag steered a new course: "Luke's got a good voice. He could do the narration."

Ruth smiled, tolerant and wise. "Oh yes? And as soon as he was up there, you'd be wanting to do it yourself."

Luke scanned the audience. The preliminary entertainments were over. There had been mimes to music composed and played by Amy, poetry reading from Adrienne, skits on various current themes at home and abroad, juggling from Ruth, unaccompanied folk-songs from Luce, a repeat performance of the afternoon's extempore drama by the youngsters of Wynster Bridge and lots of audience-involving games and competitions.

All day Luke had expected something to go wrong. The killing of the badgers he read as a sign that the hunters would return. It's been so quiet. But then, that's common sense on their part. They don't want bad publicity. They've kept their cool. Done nothing, and made us look pretty stupid.

"You'll see," Petra had said. "They'll come for us."

"Then what?"

"I've not thought that far ahead."

Perhaps as well. Fingers crossed. That old Chinese proverb got things right – please, Lord, let me live in uninteresting times. All round him, friendly faces. He probed the shadows beyond and behind.

Nothing.

Which was strange. He was suddenly more attentive to the spaces enclosing the audience: where have all the cops gone? That's marvellous. They bung up the place all day, when it's dark, they go off duty. He blinked. It was difficult to realise the difference. One minute they were there, in their usual clusters, with Alsatians; the next, melted into shadow.

The badger family must have felt the same way about me – where was I when I was needed? Sulking at home. And if there's trouble now, would I be just as useless?

"Good luck, Pete!"

"Thanks, partner." She climbed the ladder up Ron's scaffold version of the Mellport Stone, Luke's Frost Demon. "What if this thing takes a run for the river?"

"I told you, the wheels are locked. Get up there, the world awaits your message!"

So many doubts. I want to be a journalist not a dramatist. The play's no good. Corny. Too long. No shape. The words are wooden. Oh stuff it. The world awaits. You're on.

Twenty feet above the audience, Petra was glad to be concealed by grey folds of painted plastic sheeting that imitated the rippled surface of the gritstone rockstack. Ingenious old Ron, when he puts his mind to it.

He had draped swags of oak across the rock and sprays of fern and holly. On the platform, which would eventually allow a spotlight to encircle Petra's head and shoulders, there was a hook on the scaffold pole, a torch on the hook and a neat shelf for her copy of her play. Thinks of everything.

From her high nest, Petra watched the audience. It was full of people she had grown to like. Hope I don't let you down. And one in particular where fondness had deepened into something else. Yet the Sisters don't want him. "Nothing personal," Ruth had said, "but we just feel it wouldn't work." Luce: "We've one bloke too many already."

So come Monday, it's adieu.

Adrienne had voted with the others: "If you're in love with him, that would make things worse. No favourites – that's our motto, remember." What do I do? I love this life; couldn't bear this country quiet for long. Yet I'm never going to meet anyone like him again. After all, I never have.

"You want to change the world, Pete," Adrienne had said. "Luke's content with it the way it is." True, that's how it was. But Luke's altered. He's been driven out of his beloved hills, and out of a state of shock at Vera leaving.

The fact is, Luke's the one coming out of his chrysalis.

Ron had cast his vote with Petra: "I could do with help keeping this three-wheel circus on the road. Luke doesn't mind getting his mitts dirty. When you chat to him, you realise he's far from a country bumpkin . . . What he needs is a chance to escape from his pretty picture on the wall."

Petra had accepted the vote without protest, sensing the rift which had opened between herself and the others. It's time I slipped anchor too, went my own way. Nothing can be the same again. The vote had, somehow, extinguished the magic.

The audience was still, silent, expectant; so silent that a breeze off the river could be heard among the willows and alders. Up here, Petra felt coolness penetrating the last heat of the day.

It was the whisper of autumn.

"Wish me well, Luke." She reached for her playscript and found something next to it on the shelf – Luke's pine cone.

Chapter 10

Music from the dark. An old, much-loved tune danced up from the river, beaming out of loudspeakers which, in the dusk, resembled ancient standing stones:

> If you go down in the woods today,
> You're sure of a big surprise . . .

An amber spotlight outlined a shape trundling forward between billows of silver mist.

Luke grinned. The audience laughed, recognising a preacher's pulpit paint-sprayed with the words THE RED REVEREND and underneath, half-scribbled, JESUS VOTED COMMUNIST – OKAY? On the sill of the pulpit was a row of paint tins. From murky depths emerged ear-cuffing snores, and with each snore there was a peal of church bells.

Snore: clang. Snore: clang.

Petra, in a halo of white light, high in the woods: "The Reverend Rip Van Wallock-Winkle, who fell asleep in the middle of his last sermon – greetings! Welcome back to your beloved Woonster-Over-Poison."

Snore: clang. Snore: clang.

The audience spotted a naked foot protruding from the pulpit, with a large balloon tied to the big toe, and ZZZZ! written in luminous paint.

Silhouettes drifted through green floodlights – the forest in majestic gyration. Thirty young dancers, coached by Adrienne, wove patterns across yellowed grass, bearing leaf sprigs in each hand, their heads crowned with aspen.

The forest flowed as if it were both trees and water, the meandering Wynster, the wind-tousled surface of Boldventure Lake.

Suddenly, a volcanic roar from the Mellport Stone. The dancers froze, heads bent, arms and legs steel-rod straight, and the music was engulfed by the thunder of drums.

Up tottered Adrienne as the Reverend Rip, sporting a vicar's dog-collar made from the tyre of a Mini and painted white. Donkey's ears stuck through a pointed nightcap. She held a school-crossing lollipop inscribed with an exclamation mark. She spoke:

"And as I was saying before being so rudely knocked on the bonce by a lump of calcite from the congregation, we must pra . . . y for the miners – all thirty-three and a third of them who are left."

From the rear stalls beside the sentinel hawthorn, Madge with her very own part as Official Heckler:

"Twenty-one, Reverend, at the last count. Where've you been all these years?"

Reverend Rip: "Pra . . . y for the Poooooor!"

Official Heckler: "All fifty-five millions of em!"

To the accompaniment of another burst of thunder, the Frost Demon (Ruth on stilts) disengaged himself from the grey-walled rockstack tower, earning a round of applause for his resemblance to a recently-ignited sparkler. His head was spiked with glistening icicles, body herring-boned with blue and emerald ice, hands shining with ice-knife fingers, nails scratching rainbows in the floodlights.

Petra: "Behold, the Frost Demon, who once-upon-a-dream terrorised the land – the mastermind who gave the world cork-tips and *Star Wars*; who ate trade unions with coconut crunchies for breakfast . . . He was so wicked they made him Home Secretary and he brought in the death penalty for spelling mistakes."

Reverend Rip: "My son Dozy Jack put an end to

that, ladies and gentlemen." A dancer whirled across the stage, in and out of spotlight, wielding a red fire bucket, pretending to drop it, catching it, pretending to spill it, holding back at the last moment.

The dancer completed a wild pirouette by stamping on the Frost Demon's foot, sending the monster howling in a ring of sparks.

Petra: "By challenging the Frost Demon to a riddle . . ."

Frost Demon (Ruth ten feet off the ground): "Then it's a bargain, young sir. If I can guess what's in your puny, paltry, pestiferous bucket, I'm free to swab you, and swallow with kebab and custard the whole population from the Rising Sun to the Fisherman's Rest?"

Dozy Jack was prevailed upon to give the Demon a clue: what was in his bucket was in short supply and was woth a million pounds a spoonful.

Frost Demon: "The black one in a packet of fruitgums?"

A deafening "No" from the audience.

Demon: "A tin of Monarch paint the week after next? Equal pay for the women at Ecclestone's?" Each time the chorus of nos from the audience grew louder. "Councillor Smartwell's silence?"

Having failed to guess the riddle, the Frost Demon was driven back towards his rock by the dancers, chanting "In, in, in you go, Demon of Darkness. Never escape till you have guessed the riddle!"

Petra: "Touch the stone, Dozy Jack. Make the land safe. One touch at Winter Solstice, one at Summer Solstice. Then all that is required is to remember . . . remember the past!"

The ballet that followed told of forgetfulness, at first in good times, then in bad times.

Petra: "The days of fun passed; in their misery, the people turned in on themselves. They forgot how far they had come. They even forgot each other . . . And poor Dozy

185

Jack forgot to touch the stone. He dozed when he should have been vigilant."

Once more the Demon stepped from his grim rock. There was a spear of lightning in his hand which he hurled into the centre of the forest. The lightning became a river, luminous and hypnotic, drawing to it all the creatures of the greenwood. They knelt and drank, and instantly were in terrible pain. They danced to their agony as Amy's plaintive viola rose and fell like winter wind between the hills.

Luke was fascinated by the stage-effects of Ron the Wizard. I'd like a go. He glanced at the audience. He became aware of people moving, away to his left, where River Meadow sloped and flattened into Town Bottom. Yet, like Dozy Jack, he was lulled by the pine-scent of the play.

Reverend Rip: "The worst bit of my nightmare was having to listen to my own voice warning people to sit up and take notice. Warning them till the crack of doom."

Yes, people moving, yards away from the audience, but along its perimeter. Luke's attention remained fixed upon the stage.

"Crack of Doom, sir?" In a shimmer of black and white stripes, King Badger (Luce with stooped back and stumbling gait) rose out of the mist. "I fear your church clock must have stopped, dear Reverend – for all of us, the midnight chime has already struck."

Reverend Rip: "Good grief – and I forgot to take a collection!"

King Badger: "I am the ghost of Wildlife Past."

Reverend Rip: "From Luke-warm wood?"

Badger: "Sadly, good sir, there is no wood to make Lukewarm . . . It is now called Strontium Plaza. You see, there was no one to touch the stone."

"But how?" The word was taken up by the dancers

strewn beside the poisoned river: "How? how?"

The music returns:

> Beneath the trees
> Where nobody sees . . .

The attention of the audience was switched across stage. A rear-projected slide came up on Ron's giant screen situated opposite the Mellport Stone. It was a picture of Wynster Bridge from Town Moor.

Petra: "This is how Woonster's happy valley looked before the Crack of Doom." Up came more slides in quick parade: the river entering woods, reflecting willows and white clouds. "Where lovers touched toes in cool glades, where dippers dipped, skippertails skipped, but where all wasn't well with the world."

The slides speeded up: Furmiston Forest, with regiments of pine, sharply sunlit; the razor-wire fence with concrete stanchions; the gate, the guardhouse; a guard just in frame, shotgun broken at the barrel.

Petra: "And the secret cargoes that enter the forest . . ."

Pictures of the container lorries passing through the gate, first from a distance, then in close-up; one of the vehicle's registration plate, magnified in size, the letters and figures assuming a strange power like undeciphered script; like hieroglyphics, thought Luke, on a pharoah's tomb: what secrets might it unlock?

> If you go down in the woods today,
> You'd better not go alone . . .

Don't show the slides: who said that?

Reverend Rip: "Beware of the forest, my friends – watch out for the fence!"

Once more, Luke checked on the response of the

audience. It was rapt and wide-eyed. His eye lingered and this time he saw figures standing head-to-knee in white, some hooded, others wearing masks.

He turned back. Part of the show. Like the old mummers. Or in that film – can't remember. It's what this street theatre's all about – participation. Getting the locals in on the act.

I think.

Petra: "This is what happens deep in the forest . . ."

On screen, photos of the inner fence; of the billets; the floodlight pylons; the earthmovers; the mammoth yellow crane; the strange protective gear of the workers.

Don't show the slides: Stacey. The men you're tangling with kill for money.

If you go down in the woods today,
You'd better go in disguise . . .

Petra: "The temple of the future arises . . ."

Pictures of the container lorries being unzipped; of the distant concrete bunker; of the crane being fitted through steel chains; of the prize within wrappers, glistening under the lights.

"The Crack of Doom started here, Reverend Rip. Tons of deadly treasure. Alpha-beta-gamma deadly. You can't see it, smell it or touch it – but it penetrates concrete. Tipped down every hole and quarry, every moorland fissure, every creeping crevice. Washed by underground streams full of brine.

"Strewn over every salt-sea bottom beneath every shelving rock. Under the earth's crust is Poison Pie."

The figures to Luke's left began to move in slow step. Mummers, do they wear hoods? They carried unlit torches. Like soldiers sloping arms, they held short poles dressed in red and white streamers and tied with balloons.

One torch took fire. Its flame was passed along the row to the others. Luke was cold stone like the Frost Demon. "No scientist," Petra was saying, her voice binding the audience in tense silence, "has yet invented a container for this deadly treasure which resists corrosion, or damage from earth movements, for more than fifteen or twenty years."

Picture of a vast underground storage facility, piled high with steel drums, followed by another – taken from a photograph in a book – of leaking drums.

"What's safe today will be an unacceptable threat to life in the future . . ."

Luke was on his feet, the play ignored. Across the auditorium the torches of the second row of figures had been lit. He watched the mummers, still half decided that is what they were. Dad mentioned them. You should have read Pete's script, then you'd know. They were facing inwards, motionless, torch flames almost still.

He was invaded by signs. You won't read them, will you?

The slides continued. The Reverend Rip's warning was anguished: "Beware of the fence, good people!" Yet the townsfolk, strolling and chatting through the silver mist, heard nothing.

Petra: "Alas it is too late. The fence has long since surrounded the people. They do not even know it is there."

Mummers, my eye! Luke broke through the spell of wanting things to be other than they were. He ignored the fancy balloons, the red and white streamers.

Those are baseball bats.

From the Frost Demon, a shivering laugh. A cold white light had transformed the dancers into concrete posts, their oak crowns into coils of barbed wire.

Luke's heart was not beating loud enough to drown the laughter of the Frost Demon who had stepped from his rock. He too clutched balloons; an assortment of yellow and red and blue, each painted with a big black letter.

For seconds Luke was trapped in his own rock — of indecision.

The Demon strode on giddy stilts towards the audience, towering over the giggling children in the front rows. "Now what can be the meaning of Dozy Jack's riddle? What could he be carrying in his red bucket which is worth a million quid a slurpful?"

Do something, you dozy jack. Eventually Luke shook himself into movement. He turned away from the audience. He made room in the dark before circling towards the stage.

You should call the police. Is there time, and would they bother to come?

Frost Demon: "Now all you furry creatures, what do you reckon this jumble of letters adds up to? Will you help a friendly old Demon?"

"NO!" bellowed the audience.

Madge: "On yer bike, Demon!"

Frost Demon: "Okay, a deal. I'll climb back into my sarcophagus, even if it means a bout of sigh-attica, if you'll give me a teeny bit of help to put these letters in order."

Luke had acted. But where had it got him? Here I am backstage with nobody but the river to talk to. The slides continued to show the dumping operation. He hesitated beside the scaffold ladder. She'll scorch me off if I disturb her.

And if I don't?

Frost Demon: "There's N, there's P, there's T and I and O. There's double U, and Me . . ." He waddled, sky-high in front of the audience, waving balloons.UL-POM, is it?"

"UNI-UMPLOT?"

Louder: "No!"

Petra: "Should we give the Demon a clue?"

"Ye-e-s!"

"Here goes, then:" on screen, the four-spoke symbol for radiation, and below it in white letters, DANGER.

Demon: "I'm no nearer."

"One more go, then."

Luke had been snarled away by an uptight Ron. "Get out from backstage. We're busy!"

"We've trouble, Ron."

The genius of lights and sounds was not listening. "It's bad luck – so bugger off!" His voice was loud enough for the audience to hear, but they were too involved in instructing the Demon to heed the off-stage dialogue.

"P," they cried.

Luke refused to be fobbed off: bad luck's jabbing us in the eyes. "At least listen, Ron – have you got mummers with torches in the play?"

"Luke, no one, not even the Royal Family gets to talk to me when there's a performance on."

"Mummers?" insisted Luke. "Because there are twenty-odd of them out there, wearing hoods and masks. And mummers don't usually carry baseball bats."

Ron was attentive. "Not in the play, that's for sure." He went on with his work, controlling the sound, switching the slides. "Course, it could be Wynster Athletic – the whole team wanted Pete to write them into the script."

U had followed L.

"PLUSH?" guessed the Frost Demon.

"No!"

"Try again."

"T? PLUT – that's not a word."

"O."

"You mean Donald Duck's Pluto?"

Luke had moved back across the rear of the stage. His one concern was Petra. He glanced about him: there's nothing, not even a balloon to defend her with. He stood at the foot of the Mellport Stone beside the ladder. She was concealed from Luke's view by a platform of planks.

They'd not break up a whole show ... not in full view of the audience. Would they?

"Not Pluto – Plutarch?"

"No – N."

"No N?"

"Yes – N!"

"Make your minds up, you cornbrains."

"I ..."

"I? Do you mean Me?"

"No – I."

Petra: "Nearly there!"

Audience: "U."

"Me?"

"No – U."

"That doesn't makes sense."

"YES IT DOES!"

"Mm, well."

"You got it! M."

"I can't read it. You spell it out for me."

"P-L-U-T-O-N-I-U-M – plutonium!"

"Ooh, n-n-n-naughty!" The Demon stepped into a whirlpool of smoke. Betraying his promise, he held up the red bucket. He waded in among the dancers, shaking the contents of the bucket over them, over the forest creatures, and the stuff seemed to spark on the earth.

Every stage light was extinguished save for the glowing white rectangle of the screen; and this was the moment the mummers chose to attack.

They came from left to right of the audience, torches flaring, in step – quite a spectacle, creating an atmosphere that was both comical and fearful.

They marched towards the stage.

Petra: "Down in the woods tonight, the teddy bears

hold their Plutonium Picnic ... Who knows the truth of it?" The forest flashed up on the screen. In close-up was the concrete bunker. "Witness, the Holy of Holies, the twentieth century's own temple of the mysteries. Who can we rely on to tell us even half the truth?"

The assault was under way. Luke was caught on his heels. No time, no space. The mummers had followed his own route, moved outside the audience's line of attention. He saw torches expanding before him, the grimacing masks, the hoods with slit eyes.

Wrong again: not baseball bats but pickaxe handles.

They enveloped him, flames, hooded faces, blows. He was driven aside. When he twisted to rise, he was kicked. Alone. He tumbled. He was struck, a blow aimed at the head but deflected by upraised arm across shoulder and back.

What had Pete's dad said?

He heard:

"Get the girl – shut her up!"

Petra: "And now to meet the guardians of the temple." She suddenly felt the Mellport Stone being shaken. She glanced down, tried to go on: "And behind the guardians . . ."

Across stage, the second formation of mummers, wielding their balloon-tied clubs and their torches, faced the audience. They sang:

> "Heigh-ho, heigh-ho!
> It's off to work we go!"

The dwarfs' song from *Snow White*.

> "We work all day, and never play,
> Heigh-ho, heigh-ho!"

They deceived the audience into accepting this interruption as part of the play. The rocking of the rock was part of the play. The fire that seized hold of the plastic rock-face belonged to the performance. So did the fall of the Frost Demon.

Ruth crashing to earth from her stilts was greeted with cheers and applause: after all, isn't that what is supposed to happen to baddies?

Victorious over the Frost Demon, the mummers transferred attention to the Reverend Rip. His pulpit was shaken, spun, wrenched apart, while each attempt by Adrienne to escape was thwarted by pick handles and torch flames.

Now the mummers danced. Half the audience continued to laugh and applaud; half subsided into doubt, for the screen was alight. It burned the picture of the dinosaur crane beside the temple dome of the bunker, dissolving all in shadow and smoke.

Petra through the microphone: "Help everybody – help!" She was holding tenaciously on to the rock which shuddered and shifted its ground. The brakes had been released. Her voice died simultaneously with the music as the amplification system was destroyed.

A few in the audience were on their feet, but dumbstruck, still in a dream of the play, half convinced that the vicious turn of events was part of the drama.

Yet the flames were real . . .

The ladder to Petra's platform had fallen, leaving her stranded in the sky. Luke rolled under the blows of three attackers. He doubled back, rose, pitched himself head first into one mummer, bringing him down.

The others laid off for precious seconds to let the wrestlers disentangle themselves. A hood and knee-length robe proved an impediment.

Luke kicked free, reached the ladder.

Petra was yelling for attention. The flames were scaling the tower. The mummers were a wall before Luke. Holding the ladder across his chest, he fenced with each end. He caught one assailant across the head.

In return, he cried out as a pick handle was thrust into his ribs.

Other mummers were pushing the Mellport Stone, shunting it towards the river and *The Lucky Dragon*. Luke grasped the ladder at the narrow end. He swung it round him with such force that he cleared a passage to the scaffold.

"Pete!"

Over went the tower. People from the audience had started to come down. They were driven away. "Out – back!"

"Luke!"

Over. The blazing rock was over, tilting, almost gone. And they made the last push a charge. Over.

In the stomach, this blow. Luke buckled. Keep moving. Through arms. Felt blows, ignored them. Wild, but going down. The tower of rock, the tower of flames, now leaned out, across water, but also across the stem of *The Lucky Dragon*.

Petra could not hold. She saw Luke vanishing under clubs. She screamed, but the voice carried no distance. She was going backwards. Dark water. The stars were all shooting stars. She lost her grip. The momentum of the falling tower launched her into space – close, tight, short.

"Christ Almighty!"

Luke had gone under, awaited the finish-off. Yet he was abandoned. The mummers had seen Petra fall, topple towards water, but not quite far enough. She hit the barge roof, her cry silenced.

She rolled into the river.

"Let's get out of here!" Don's command. "Now lads!" The mummers turned tail, opened out from the kill, leaving Luke spreadeagled in grass. They fled along the river bank, casting their torches into the water.

The on-stage mummers rounded off their handiwork with a deep bow and made their exit stage-right. They smashed everything round them, and the ultimate target – once Adrienne, Amy, Luce and Ruth had been clubbed aside – was *The Lucky Dragon*.

They had weapons for the task: bottles filled with petrol were lobbed at the barge. Torches followed.

Luke had received a hit under his nose. It bled. His ears burned. He could stand, but swayed. He could hardly see. All he knew was – Pete's in the river. His legs moved in tiny shaking paces. Now he saw the barge alight. Already the smoke was billowing thickly in every direction.

Got to run. Can't run. He was at the stern of the barge. He should jump. "Pete!" He stumbled on board, stepped over flames. Here? Where else? No sign. Bloody smoke! He stared and was blind.

"Pete?"

Now. He slipped into water.

The river was gentle here, shallow enough to walk not swim. She was entangled in him, but not holding, not moving. Out. Head up, but too deep to give her air.

"Luke!" Alfred emerged through smoke, and Ron was beside him. "Heave her up – steady!" They held her. "You too." He climbed, saw nothing but fire.

They were on the bank. No need for lights, the whole barge roof was ablaze.

Ron: "She's not breathing. She's swallowed – "

"Get her away from the fire!"

Choked on smoke, get away, over, on to grass; rushed on now by more assistants – Bill Gordon and two St John's Ambulance men.

The hunters had burst through the crowd, striking out at anyone daring to step in their path. *The Lucky Dragon* exploded, sending plumes of fire into the night sky. Its grand finale was reflected in the river and caught in blistering profile against the backdrop of willows.

Petra was eased on to jackets laid on the grass. Helpers jostled to give assistance. She was lifted on to her side by one of the St John's Ambulance men. His fingers loosened her tongue, and the river tricked from her mouth.

Luke had only one thought: is she breathing? He was held back by Alfred and Ron. "An ambulance is coming . . . so let the St John's people do it, Luke."

"I know what to do!" Yet he was trembling so violently, he would probably snap her bones if he touched her. He wouldn't be forced away from her side, though. He watched the St John's men. They stooped over Petra who had been moved on to her back. There was blood on her forehead, blood in the river-drenched hair. "Is she breathing?"

The first man leant close, covered Petra, listened: plainly nothing.

Luke could wait no longer. "Thump her chest – you've got to . . ."

The man raised a cautionary hand to Luke. He knew what had to be done. His back became a barrier between Luke and Petra.

"And breathe into her!" Luke's face was dissolving. The head had produced the sweat which had opened up his own wound. He wiped the blood away – but it was also tears. The blow wasn't hard enough. He knew. "Oh come on – come on!"

Alfred, tender, yet stern: "Steady, Luke."

"She's only seconds."

The ambulanceman shifted his position. He propped up Petra's head with his left hand. With his right, he pinched her nostrils. He lowered his face to her open mouth, and blew slowly but firmly into it. He raised his glance. He repeated the action: breathe, wait, look.

The other St John's man had covered Petra with coats. He stood up. "The rest of you will need treatment." He approached Luke whose nose looked worse than it was. He held out his palms to make buffers.

"I'm all right." His eyes were on Petra, on the patient ambulanceman. "Is she?" Now he broke from Alfred's grasp. He knelt on the other side of Petra. He stared into her face, glistening, at the closed eyes; at the ambulanceman. "Please – let me have a go."

"Luke – come back here!"

Yet the ambulanceman agreed. "We must keep on . . . There's nothing so far."

Luke saw black and red, darkness and flames, the crowd huddled around him. He squatted over Petra. "You're not going to die on us!" He was angry. He pressed his hand to her sternum. His anger was not at her, but it was reflected in the blow he struck.

Then he knelt beside her, arched her neck. He put his hand under her, held it. He brushed wet hair from a freckled forehead. There was blood in her sandy brows. More a bad graze than a direct blow. He pinched her nose tightly. He bent, with full lungs, pressed his mouth to hers and blew deeply, long.

He held, watched, waited, blew.

"Come on!" He was almost shouting. "Pete . . ." He bowed his head, blew, waited. He could not see for tears and sweat, and some blood from the knock behind the ear which had trickled forward to his chin. "Pete, it's Luke – come on!" His blood fell on her. He wiped it away with tissues thrust in his hand by Adrienne. He stopped. He sucked in air. He blew, firmly, and he felt her lips were warm.

A sudden spasm of joy: he thought he saw her chest move. He pressed his lips to hers. He blew, deep, willing the life back into her. He paused, observed.

"I think . . ." He watched for the movement. "Yes – oh God, make it yes!"

The St John's man was nodding. "She's breathing." The words rippled round the crowd.

Breathing!

A great swell of emotion spread through faces and hearts. They heard Luke shout "Come on, Pete!" He bent again, blew, waited. The breathing was there. He yelped. His tears were now threatening to do what the river had not quite managed to do. He accepted another clutch of tissues. He wiped Petra's face, he wiped his own.

"My turn, son," said the St John's man. This time Luke did not round on him. He let the man take his place. He found it difficult to get to his feet and Alfred helped him.

"See, Dad?"

Dad saw.

The siren of the ambulance cut through the hushed murmurs of River Meadow. The crowd formed a route to Petra; and the headlights of the ambulance illuminated the final scene of Pete's play. The driver and mate spoke few lines. They acted without fuss. Petra was carried off-stage and aboard the ambulance. Oxygen was administered to her.

The second St John's man ushered forward Adrienne and Ruth. He had cleaned their wounds. "Shock," he said. "They'd better come with you." Nods. Luke was not invited, did not press his case. He watched the doors close on Petra.

He was thinking about the road over to Rowmanton, the great Switchback, full of potholes. "Will she be okay?"

Alfred had him by the shoulder. "Let them mop you up, Luke."

"I'm all right, Dad. Okay . . . Thanks."

"Do as I say – please!" Alfred clasped his son's neck. Luke felt a soaked cloth pressed to his forehead. The cool douse and the rhythm of firm wipes soothed him. He looked up. *The Lucky Dragon* would not survive. Everything was being consumed, a fireball no brigade could bring under control.

This is the price you pay.

Luke's eyes flickered across the carnage, then stopped. They focused. He saw Pete's Norton Navigator beneath the trees, unharmed, waiting patiently on its stand, seeming to say – who needs me?

"Luke – you're not finished."

He was feverish again. He backed off from treatment. "Later."

"Where're you going?"

"Rowmanton."

"Not in your state."

Luke indicated the Navigator. "I'm going."

"No!"

"Push off, Dad – get things sorted."

Alfred did as he was told. He held back the St John's men. "Let him be!"

Luke's short-cut to the Rowmanton road circled beneath the Winter Hill. It joined the old forest road from Stepback. The hot air, parted into a semblance of wind by the speed of the Navigator, dried his head yet reminded him he was soaked to the skin; cold skin. The route was etched on his brain. He hardly bothered to look ahead of him: a homing pigeon that knows but one destination.

I was so useless. Why didn't I shout the alarm much sooner?

His route dipped, lurched right – and was blocked at the junction. A passenger coach had reversed up the lane. Lights were on. There was no through way. On one side of the coach was a ditch and a dry-stone wall, on the other a crowd climbed aboard.

Wait.

But can't wait; won't wait. Yet he did, until a message struck his fuddled senses: those are the mummers. Those.

There was jubilant celebration: cheering, all talking and shouting at once; re-enactments of victory blows. Bottles smashed against the wall. The coach operators were Eddingworth of London.

All this way to destroy the enemy? To silence one little Pete? Luke waited only long enough for the last man to step on the bus. He freewheeled down the slope. At the last instant he had to swerve outwards.

Don Neeson had stepped from the coach.

Luke wrenched the machine into the dry ditch. He kick-started the engine. He zoomed out of the ditch, skidded on cinders at the lane end.

Don had recognised him. He raced after him, shouting. The driver's door of the Landcruiser, parked in front of the coach, was open and ready. "We've been bloody followed!" Don crashed the gears. Paddy, Sandy, Cheekburns and Luigi were sharing a crate of strong ale.

"What's the rush, Don?"

The Landcruiser accelerated at such a speed, and then braked with such suddenness, that Luigi was pitched over the front seat. "Get out – all of you! There's too much weight."

Paddy, Sandy and Cheekburns obeyed; Luigi successfully pleaded to remain. "Is fun, eh, Don?"

Luke dropped his head down, almost to the bars. He was desperate. Too many staights between here and Rowmanton. The Norton won't hold, not against the

Landcruiser. Even on the bends, she's slower. Must be me. Both of us need a decoke. In a daze, slowing down, can't seem to make ground.

I can hear them. In the mirror, road behind clear. Then a bend, the angle of the hills, hedges – and Don Neeson's beam lights hit the sky. Too open: ahead, half a mile of pure acceleration. Got to get off here. Finished otherwise.

Luke braked, steered the Navigator into a lane which ran almost in the opposite direction to Rowmanton. Yet narrow. They'll have to slow, lose revs.

The woods above were soon the woods below. Through cow dung, crossed-tracks, grass growing between the tarmac. Head ringing. I'm not really in control. He felt something. A splash of rain. Impossible. It'll never rain again. Imagination. Then a second drop, spreading; a drop against his mouth.

Trouble is, mind won't work. In shock. Why bother with me? Only one bend behind. A maniac. Even these narrow lanes won't help me, not if he's mad. And every second of this stupidity keeps me from Pete. I'd die and she'd never know.

And if she dies while I . . .

Flashing lights from the van. No joke. No competition. No drunken tractor driver to come to the rescue this time with a ton of hay bales.

In Don's cab, silence, Luigi holding on, eyes burning. "Avanti! Avanti!"

"Sure – avanti! What's it mean?"

"Forward march!"

Suddenly clear of everything but walls, most of them broken. All the world was below, sunken. There, deep and deeper south, the river. Where we swam, Pete, last century. "Am I or am I not dumpy?" Oh Jesus. Soaring up. Taking flight into black wind and rain. Yes, autumn at last screeching across the hills.

They're going to kill me, Pete.

The high bank dropped away. The ditch levelled, flattened at the approach to the five-barred gate which opened into the kingdom of the Frost Demon. No choice. Luke swerved right, scraping the stile post.

The Landcruiser could not manoeuvre the angle. It collided with stone. Metal jarred, caught, cracked. Neeson enjoyed the difficulty. He reversed and capsized into the opposite ditch, metal striking stone once more. But tyres gripped, held.

"Got him!"

To intruders upon the privacy of the Frost Demon, this meadow was without dimension. The rain-clouds had eclipsed the stars, robbed Don of any clues as to how far the land stretched, whether up or down, or any hint of the surface beneath his wheels – ploughed soil, grass or stubble.

No clues save one: a single eye of light fifty yards away, enclosed in featureless dark. "He thinks he can double back on us." Don Neeson's foot hovered above the accelerator.

"Bloody nerve! Like the bullfight, eh, Don? To-re-a-dor!"

Don had his instructions, his orders from above, but they were not the reason that made him hesitate.

"Kill him, Don!"

"Like we killed his girl?"

"Avanti!"

Luke shook with terror, but his memory continued to put data on record: Pete, you lost another earring. The Landcruiser was large as the sky. "Come on, what's keeping you?" His back was to the quarry edge. Beyond, in space, stood the Frost Demon. The Navigator was roasting. Rain steamed off its pipes. Don't cut out on me now.

His head was going like fireworks. Don will charge.

With luck, Luke would slip out of his path. He waited
– and waited. "Oh hell . . ."

To Luigi's amazement, Don Neeson had switched off
the ignition of the Landcruiser. He was staring ahead of
him at the enticing light.

"Why you not get him, Don?"

"Your trouble, Luigi, is that you don't read enough – "

"Read? Che cosa! What you say, read?"

Don opened his door. He stepped into the darkness. He
stood in the periphery of his light beam. The wind bristled
off the moor. The rain slanted and sparkled through the
light. He called:

"Okay, son. Think yourself lucky this time!"

Luke did not need inviting twice; but he was neither
cowed nor grateful. He passed within ten yards of the
Landcruiser, almost halted beside it:

"And you think yourself lucky!"

Luigi was bawling at Don to get back into the van.
Instead, he found his door opened. He was yanked out
into the rain. "We're taking a walk, Luigi."

"I no want walk!"

"You walk." Don frog-marched him forward. "Avanti!
Now look."

The void opened at Luigi's feet. "Je-sus Christ!"

"Capisci – understand?"

"Io capisco bene, Don."

"Clever son-of-a-bitch. He was right. We should count
ourselves lucky."

"But how?"

"The redhead's diary, Luigi – remember?"

"I no read . . ."

"Very poetic. And it described this place. I should
have guessed he'd come here. She called it their trysting
place."

"Trysting?"

"Where lovers meet."

"Why you give up chase, Don?"

Don's gaze had strayed towards the Frost Demon. "We'd have hit it slap in the middle, and the boulder on top would have crushed us."

"For that, he die, va bene? Come on, Don – presto!"

Don Neeson made no effort to follow Luigi back to the van. The Italian turned, snappy at the prospect of losing his prey. "Now and again," said Don wearily, "I wish I kept better company. You, Luigi . . . kill for fun. Va bene. But me, I like to get paid."

"You wanted him!"

"My temper wanted him. That wasn't professional."

Luigi kicked a stone towards the quarry edge. He was nodding, his own fury abated. "You have the doubts, Don, eh? This whole job."

"Maybe."

"The play – you listen her, the redhead?" Don did not reply. Luigi grinned. "At least this boy, he learn the lesson, is true?"

It was the closest Don Neeson ever got to a real smile. "You want a bet?" They returned through the beams of the Landcruiser. Don was in no hurry to drive off. "It's because there are people like us, Luigi, that there'll always be people like him, and his girl . . . We make the cash, but they make the hope."

Rowmanton Hospital. Luke Waller raced from the forecourt to Casualty Reception. The waiting-room was full, but there was no one at the desk.

"Anybody around?" There was no response; a glance or two, then averted eyes, all sunk in English patience and resignation. Get in the queue. "Well, thanks anyway."

I'm dripping over the floor. The motion of the Navigator still throbbed through his limbs. He was dizzy. Can't hang about. He turned, went down a pale corridor in the direction of the wards.

"Doctor?"

"Not me, pal, I'm the 'umble porter round here."

"A girl – a redhead, brought in with . . . please?"

"Try Casualty."

"Nobody there."

"They'll be back. Be patient – here, not down there!"

Luke blazed: "This is an emergency!" He had darted past the porter, who was too old to catch him or pursue him.

"You're not permitted in here." A nurse at the entrance to Ward One.

"Petra Scales – brought in about an hour ago?"

"Go to Casualty. And you need mopping up yourself."

Yes, he was bleeding again. Shouldn't have scratched it; and the River Wynster was irrigating the polished tiles. "Beggar Casualty – they're on holiday." He ran. Halfway down the wide passage, he stopped, hearing a lift arrive from an upper floor. Two white-coated figures were bringing a patient on a trolly.

Pete, oh Christ!

The patient was completely covered by a white sheet. The lift doors slid noisily open. They were passing.

Luke cried "Please!" He lifted the sheet.

"What the – "

The face wasn't Petra's. It was that of an elderly man. "Sorry – so sorry!" He scattered. Almost at Casualty Reception again, he glanced down a green avenue of doors. One was marked X-RAY.

The receptionist was calling him. The porter was beside her. "I'm sorry but it's strictly forbidden to – "

"Petra Scales, answers to Pete . . . Redhead, injured. A bad fall. One blue john earring." He almost made himself laugh, and though it was not quite a laugh, it reduced the tension in him. He was exhausted. "I must know!"

A doctor whitened a space in the corner of Luke's vision. "You must be Luke."

He sprang round and was held in a grip which seemed to presage terrible news. "You need treatment."

"Pete?"

The doctor beckoned him towards X-Ray, to an anteroom. "You can see her for two minutes."

"Then . . ." He was in a trance. Luke, called for. Me. I was Luke. Maybe I'm still Luke. Maybe I can be Luke in future.

If.

"Is she – ?"

"Lucky, yes. Not too long . . . I've put her pals in Ward Three for the night. They're okay."

She was conscious, pale as the sheet. The pillow was aflame with her hair. And Luke took fire from her smile. "Luke?" His hands enfolded hers. He wanted to throw his arms round her. He wanted to cry. He wanted to shout the roofs off.

He couldn't speak for these dimwit tears. He tried to nod. He heard her whisper. "Everything's okay." He could not decide whether this was a question or a statement. He wanted to bury his face in her hands. Speak, damn you. The hills are becoming green again, but they will never match her eyes.

"It's . . . It's actually raining." The words ran out of him. "Raining! In England – rain. It's unbelievable!"

Petra's hand nestled in his, pudgy as they make them. "Some Gypsy Rose you make!"

He shook his head, dropped rain and river on her. He heard her say, "Luke, we'll be needing that tent after all . . ."